T0368900

TRUE BLUE

TRUE BLUE

Christopher M. Spence

TRUE BLUE

iUniverse books may be ordered through booksellers or by contacting:

iUniverse
1663 Liberty Drive
Bloomington, IN 47403
www.iuniverse.com
1-800-Authors (1-800-288-4677)

Because of the dynamic nature of the Internet, any web addresses or links contained in this book may have changed since publication and may no longer be valid. The views expressed in this work are solely those of the author and do not necessarily reflect the views of the publisher, and the publisher hereby disclaims any responsibility for them.

Any people depicted in stock imagery provided by Getty Images are models, and such images are being used for illustrative purposes only.
Certain stock imagery © Getty Images.

ISBN: 978-1-5320-9413-2 (sc)
ISBN: 978-1-5320-9414-9 (e)

Print information available on the last page.

iUniverse rev. date: 01/24/2020

Dedicated to the "at promise" young men of B2M (*Boys2Men*) Chicago and beyond. Your creativity and resiliency continues to inspire me. I am painfully aware of the disparities you face and the need to find ways to improve your life and school outcomes. My commitment is to use my platform to amplify your voice, and to cultivate your gifts using a "relationships matter" approach to become stewards of your own lives.

CHAPTER ONE

The street corner of 52nd Street and Howard Street was at the heart of the hood I grew up in. Like every other pair of streets in that slum, the concrete was dirty and stained, and the cracked walls were decorated with layer upon layer of fading graffiti; plastered with the names of a thousand different desperate youth looking for some way to put their mark on the world. A thousand different tags representing a thousand different lives; many of them taken early by gang warfare or thrown off track by the school to the prison pipeline. From that corner, you could just about see everything that the hood could cough up; like a podium where you could stand and watch the sorry world go by.

Across the street was the run down old liquor store where all the deadbeat moms and dads would gather to spend their cash after collecting their welfare. They'd go in with the money meant for their kids and come out with bottles barely disguised in familiar brown paper bags. Those brown paper bags were everywhere in the hood – you'd see them blowing across your path now and then, like tumbleweed; a reminder that you lived in a world fuelled by alcohol, drugs and lost hope.

You couldn't blame the people who lived there for feeling hopeless. We all did. The school playgrounds were as dangerous as the jail yards, and the inmates just as tough; so most of us didn't make it far. Living in the hood, it didn't matter how hard you tried to stay on track – something would trip you up, whether it was getting involved with the wrong crowd, getting shot in a drive-by or just being swallowed up by the poverty that engulfed the whole damn community.

People in the hood never seemed to walk anywhere, but shuffled; like they either didn't have the energy or the health to really put one foot in front of the other. And I guess most of them didn't.

The hood sucked all the energy out of you like this huge, ravenous void that devoured all innocence and aspiration. You started out thinking you could beat it, but then just got sucked in and dragged down by it like everyone else. I think of all those parents who said 'I'll do better for my kids', only to see their kids shot down or end up behind bars like all the others, and then there's nothing to do but drink and smoke and shuffle along.

Except for the youth of the hood. Now here were people with bodies full of pent up frustration and resentment. Some of them would let out their hatred for the world in angry, rhythmic lyrics that spilled out in rap over the blare of heavy beats on loud speakers. Others took their rage a step further, and went out looking for blood.

One of the toughest gangs would gather on 52nd Street, and their rivals on Howard Street. A lot of the time they missed each other, but if the face of a member from one gang should appear on that corner whilst the other gang was out, all hell would break loose.

I'd seen it a hundred times growing up – fists pumping, teeth flying, blood spilling, mama's crying and bodies dropping.

Sometimes when it rained, old blood would spill out of the gutters. Those gutters were filthy and overflowing with the dirt and debris of the hood – and probably a hundred thousand discarded paper bags, cigarette butts, condoms and syringes. The whole sickening mess would rise up and overflow from the gutters in bad weather, making those streets where the gangs came to make war even more treacherous.

A lot of the folk that lived in the hood were the sort of people you'd cross the street to get away from. They wore their troubles like backpacks weighing them down. They had hate in their eyes and scowls on their faces. They lived by the rules of 'dog-eat-dog' and looked out for number one, which made them dangerous people.

Yeah, I grew up around dangerous people – not that everyone in the hood was a criminal, a pimp or a dealer. Some were just ordinary folk that were down on their luck. Some were born in the hood, and others drifted there one way or another. Nobody chose to be there, that's for sure.

These were the folk who kept their heads down and kept themselves to themselves. They never got involved in the violence, but never stood up to it either. They just tried to live their lives as best they could in the squalor and depravity, and counted their blessings if they made it home from some crappy minimum wage job alive.

Most people in the hood fell into one of these two groups – the criminal or the down and out. But, there was a third type of person who came by now and then. These people were rare and rarely did well in the hood, because they represented something that was so out of reach for many – hope.

These people were those that came to the hood or stayed in the hood by choice, because they wanted to make it better. They were those who somehow didn't get drawn down into the madness, and they didn't run from it either.

They were the social workers, and the volunteers; the teachers that tried to inspire and instil self-belief in students who had been raised not to believe in much. They were the foster parents that didn't do it for the money, but that did it because they knew that too many kids were raised without love and without role models; thrown aside by the system and left to get swept up by the undercurrent and washed away into those filthy gutters of the hood.

They were the community workers, who tried to raise money for basketball courts and apprenticeships, so that kids had the choice of better ways to spend their time than fighting and stealing. They were the doctors and nurses that gave their time voluntarily in the free clinic to help the homeless pregnant and crack heads, just because nobody else would.

They were the few honest cops who weren't out to get anybody, but just wanted to make the world a safer place.

Yeah, there were good people in the hood, and transformative places like Family Matters. It took someone tough and loyal to the streets to be a hero there. You had to be in it for more than glory and more than some half-hearted notion about morals and dreams. The hood had to be in your blood if you wanted to make a change; otherwise it would sense you didn't belong there, and spit you back out.

CHAPTER TWO

Harold Washington High School was where I went to school as a kid, and in the fifteen years since I'd left it, it hadn't changed a bit. It still stood tall and concrete, looking more like a prison than a place of learning, with its grass trodden down by the shoes of countless schoolkids and back buildings covered in graffiti.

Sitting on the steps outside the building were a whole bunch of kids who were there simply because they had no place better to be. They didn't come to learn – because what could an education do for them? – but came to meet up with others like them, to try and find a sense of belonging, even if they couldn't find a sense of achievement or success.

I remembered it well; what it was like to be a student at HWHS. I used to roll up half an hour late every day and still spend an hour chilling with my boys, smoking and shooting the breeze, before finally dragging myself indoors, and only then to compete with my mates over who could cause the young, hopeless teacher to burst into tears first.

Looking back, my attitude seems pretty shocking, and maybe even a little cruel against those few teachers that really tried, but what did I care back then? Nobody I knew had an education, and nobody I knew that survived in the hood would waste their time with one. I knew that no book was going to save me from a bullet if I got on the wrong side of a gang fight one day. What I needed was street smarts and loyal friends – and I had both in spades.

Not much had changed with the kids today, it seemed. I could feel their hostility rising off their skins as I approached – a stranger in their midst. They wore the faces of bored and frustrated young people with a lot on their minds; and they only scowled when I gave a friendly smile, but I hadn't expected more than that. I knew the hood well enough to know that only do-gooders and backstabbers smiled at you – and you didn't want to associate with either. If you stuck with the do-gooders, then people would think you were soft, and you'd end up with a target on your back. If you stuck with a backstabber, then it wouldn't be long before you were the next in line for their betrayal.

The only way to survive was through a fierce loyalty to the few that you could call friends and a determination to keep your distance from everyone else. So, here, on this drizzly Wednesday morning, I didn't expect a smile from anyone, because I was a stranger and a do-gooder; a cop, here to tell these hopeless kids that they could do better.

I finished staring at the face of the building and took my first few steps inside. Not much had changed in here either. Geez, I'm pretty sure that some of those fading, peeling posters were on the walls when I went here. Graffiti everywhere. Litter. Noise. The smell of weed.

Kids were fighting in the corridors. Girls were wagging their fingers and yelling at one another by the lockers. Music was playing. Skateboards were flying, basketballs were bouncing. Even the younger kids had their hoods pulled up and suspicious looks on their faces. Some of them were far too young to look that jaded.

I headed straight to the Principal's office and Mr Branch welcomed me in. He was a balding blonde, watery-eyed white man who always looked anxious and worn-out. I'm pretty sure that I'd turned a few of those blonde hairs grey in my time due to my antics when I'd been a student here, but me and Mr Branch were cool now. I was one of his only success stories, and he was so relieved that I'd agreed to come. He held out a clammy hand and greeted me with a big, thankful grin.

"Reggie! It's so good to see you again. How have you been?"

"Good, good," I replied. "Wow. It's crazy to be back."

"How long has it been now, Reggie?"

"Oh, some fifteen years. Yep. A long time."

"It's not often any of our students finds our way back here after they graduate – unless it's to well, you know. It was good of you to come."

"How could I say no? This kind of thing was the reason I became a cop. I wanted to be an example for the next generation of kids growing up here. Now's my chance."

"I'm praying that you'll make an impact on at least one or two of them," Mr Branch said desperately. "God knows they need some inspiration in their lives – although most don't want to hear it. They're tired of false promises."

I let out a little scornful laugh and smiled wryly. "I remember. I used to be one of them."

"But something got through to you though, Reggie. You turned your life around. What was it?"

My smile faded and I felt a tug of grief deep in my stomach. "A lot more than a gym hall speech."

There they were. The faces of eight-hundred kids who'd heard it all before and didn't want to hear it again. They were bickering and fighting, and sneering and messing around with each other when backs were turned. Most of the faces were black. It made me sad to see, because those were the faces of kids who weren't engaged in their learning. They were the faces of kids who'd lost hope and forgotten how to have big dreams. It hurt to see them. Their faces showed anger, but I knew that those scowls and jeers were just the result of a deep and burning desire to just experience something *more*.

In front of me was an old microphone with a fraying wire that hissed and popped even before I started speaking into it. Those little static pops went off like gunfire from the wire mouthpiece, but the rabble of the school kids drowned it out. The rabble continued even after I started to speak.

"Good morning, students!"

No response. Maybe a couple of raised eyebrows and sets of rolling eyes, but hardly more than a sideways glance from most. I tried again.

"Uh-*hmm* –," – I cleared my throat loudly into the mic, - "I said *good morning.*"

Nothing. Time for a different tactic.

"*Listen up!*"

Shouting into the mic caused a few more faces to turn my way. I kept my tone of voice assertive and took the mic from its stand, beginning to pace up and down for effect, and speaking as loudly as I could until my voice echoed around the hall like the mighty Wizard of Oz.

"I'm here to talk to you." I said seriously. "You know why? Because kids like you get shot and stabbed and put away in jail everyday, and it's not uncommon, and it's not 'bad luck' – it's life in the hood and you could be next."

The rabble began to quiet down. Now I was talking a language that these kids could understand. The language of the streets – it wasn't pretty, and it wasn't calm and it wasn't politically correct. It was brutal and real and honest.

"Now, most of you want to roll your eyes. You're wondering what right someone like me has to come in here and tell someone like you how to live your life. Well, let me tell you something. Fifteen years ago, I was sitting where you're sitting now, listening to some do-gooder just like me, coming in here and trying to tell me how green the grass is on the other side. And like you, I sat there thinking: 'What other side?'"

"Like you, I didn't listen to him. I rolled my eyes and I chuckled and I'd had enough of hearing it. I'd had enough of people coming and telling me that I could do whatever I wanted and be whoever I wanted, because that's not real life, right? Real life is happening here in the hood, and it's not college degrees and new houses and fancy cars. It's living meal to meal, and doing what you can to get by. It's alcohol and drugs on street corners, and wondering which one of you will be the next to get shot, or even die out there. It's trying to earn respect, because what else have you got?"

"Yeah, I was like you. You know what changed it for me? Learning that a friend of mine got shot and died out on those streets, trying to get by, trying to look hard, just like you do. And where was I? On the inside. Yeah, you're not there to have anybody's back when you're in the slammer."

"It's easy to listen to a guy like me and think 'I've had enough of hearing that', but you know what I'd really had enough of at your age? I'd had enough of working my ass off to get by and looking over my shoulder all the time. I'd had enough of watching my mom work three jobs to get by. I'd had enough of the violence and the poverty. Yes, it's difficult to listen to a guy like me come in and tell you it can be better, but what you should really feel sick of is what's right around you – the real life that's happening."

"I'm here to tell you that things can change. You can do whatever you want to do. You can be whoever you want to be. You can leave the hood and live that life you think is out of your reach. Or, like me, you can come back and try your hardest to make that place better, so that one day, the 'hood' won't be here anymore."

"So yeah, you're wondering what right someone like me has to come in here and tell someone like you how to live your life. Well, you know what? I'm not going to tell you what to do, because I'm not the person to do that. But I am going to tell you one thing: If you get caught breaking the law, you're going to end up in a juvey, just like I did."

"Now, I turned it around after that, and I got to where I am – but I got lucky. Just because I got a second chance, don't expect it to happen to you. One wrong move, and it could be game over for you. Take the chance to change your life while it's there; and, if you really want to do something real, take the chance to change others' lives too. Make something of yourself and pull someone else up with you.

That's what real loyalty looks like – not picking up a gun to settle someone else's beef. Take it from me. I've been there."

It was hard to tell if I'd got through to them or not. Some kids were still scowling. Some were still rolling their eyes. But there were a few faces in that crowd that wore expressions like something I'd said had hit home; like maybe they had a desire in them to get away from here to find something better; like they wanted to be the best versions of themselves that they could be, and they were seeing proof for the first time that it could happen.

From there I went on to talk about all the other things I'd come to talk about –the community outreach program I was involved in, the Police Athletic League, how to get into the police force – and wound down with some motivational spiel that probably didn't have the same impact as my hard-hitting opening.

I finished my speech wondering if anything I'd said would have stuck, but hoping that it would. It would be a blessing if these kids could choose a better direction for their lives based on the power of a motivational speech alone, rather than having to be shaped by tragedy and wrong turns, like me.

CHAPTER THREE

There were three in my crew. Me, Winston and Leo. We did everything together. I wouldn't go so far as to say we were a gang, but we had that same kind of vicious loyalty to each other that you'd find in one. No, we weren't a gang, but we'd been our own kind of trouble.

We had quick fingers, you see. All three of us saw no harm in taking what we wanted from wherever we wanted; whether it was a pack of smokes from behind the counter at the shop on the corner, or a pack of beers from the liquor store. You see, none of us had much to our names, and we saw our poverty as a great injustice that needed to be righted. The world hadn't given us what we needed, so we took it.

Looking back, I feel real ashamed of how I used to see the world and how I acted in it. I saw my Mom working three jobs to keep us going, and my Dad being laid off time and time again from hard labour jobs and I didn't think it was fair. Why should they work that hard for so little? Everything's free if you don't get caught taking it.

Winston and Leo shared my way of thinking. Winston had parents like mine. They worked real hard to keep food on the table, which meant he saw neither of them very often, while Leo didn't have parents at all. Both his Mom and Dad were in jail for different drug crimes, which meant that he'd been passed around most of his life. He'd lived with his Grandma until she'd passed. Then he'd just been another kid going from home to home in the system. All three of us were left to our own devices, due to our parents being absent in one way or another – mine and Winston's worked every hour God sent, and Leo didn't really have anyone to watch over him. So, there we were: three angry kids with nobody watching us.

So, we did what all kids in the hood do when left to choose how to spend their time, and we got up to no good. Even now, I couldn't really tell you why I did it. I think it was a mixture of feeling like the world owed me something and wanting to show everyone around me that I was worth something.

I mean, ever since I can remember, I was the kid who could steal anything without getting caught. Whatever you wanted, I was your guy. I did it because it kept people on my side – I would get them what they needed – and I did it because I was bored and angry. And I did it because I was good at it.

My parents had tried to shove books and learning down my throat from a young age, and would constantly say things like 'Don't end up like us', but I thought they were idealists who were stupid to think that any hood kid would ever be anything more. I didn't want to stand out, either.

I grew up around tough kids and criminals, and if you weren't tough or a criminal, too, then you were different, and I didn't want to be. I wasn't a real smart kid, to be honest, and I was just as poor and down on my luck as everyone else, so when my parents were out working late and not around, it was much easier to fall in with the crowd than to keep myself to myself and work hard just because parents I hardly got time to see told me that I should. When I was growing up, I felt like Winston and Leo and all the other kids who hung out on street corners were my family and it was their opinions I cared about. It was their approval I wanted. So I did what they did, and what I had to do to fit in, and I didn't give a damn if it was right or wrong. It was just how we lived.

There was a certain thrill in it too, I guess. I remember how my heart would thump and the adrenalin would kick in every time I saw a cop drive by, because even if I wasn't stealing right that moment, I couldn't be sure that they weren't after me for something I did on any other day. Then that sense of loyalty and street pride would rear its rebellious head and I'd go running down to the corner of 52nd and

Howard to warn the hoes and druggies there that the police were on their way and watch them scatter like pigeons when you throw a stone their way. It made me feel a part of it; part of the mad rush and dirty current, always running, always chasing, always gambling, taking risks. Adrenalin came to fill all those gaps inside and make me feel alive. Because that's what we all wanted, really – to feel alive, to feel part of something. None of us were great achievers or innovators; we didn't have passions to pursue. We had each other and the streets. That was all.

Winston and Leo were good friends to have growing up. Winston was pretty serious and forward-thinking and probably would have made a good businessman if he'd have had the drive, because he had that perfect poker face and the ability to talk himself out of any trouble. Leo, on the other hand, was impulsive and reckless, and couldn't resist a sarcastic remark or rude comeback when someone rubbed him up the wrong way, so he was always beefing with someone.

And me? Well, what can I say about me, really? I wasn't smart, like I said. I wasn't astute like Winston, and I wasn't rude like Leo. I was just Reggie. Loyal. Daring. I liked the sense of danger that followed me in the hood.

One day, I'd take that love for adrenalin and danger and turn it into something good by becoming a cop myself, but back in the day, I didn't see how those bad boy traits could ever turn me into someone good. I was born and bred in the hood, and if things hadn't gone down the way they had, I'd not have been far behind Leo in dying at the barrel of a gun.

CHAPTER FOUR

I still come back to the basketball courts to this day, because that's where all the kids go, and if there's one reason that I became a cop, it was to save kids from making wrong choices. So I made a point of showing up where they'd be in my plain clothes, and playing some ball or shooting the breeze, just so they'd know me as more than just a police officer; but as a human being, too – one of them.

Today was another dreary day, but the youth still came to play ball. It was one of the few ways to spend your time in the hood that didn't involve ripping someone off or drawing blood that got you clout. I'd see the same group of kids there most the time – Andre, Devon, Ray Ray, Savion, Kevin, Derrek, Paul -, and today another kid that I'd been keeping my eye on.

His name was Lil Smooth, and there was something about him that made me feel like he needed someone watching over him. Smooth was a kid making too much of an effort to fit in. He wore the baggy pants and long vest with the cheap gold chains and other bling dripping off his fingers and around his neck. He fancied himself some rapper or a player, but he looked to me like a little kid playing dress up.

Maybe it was because he was young – fifteen, maybe sixteen at most – and scrawny. Not lean. Scrawny, like he hadn't eaten in days, although it was probably the cigarettes that kept the weight off him. Sometimes I could smell the normal kind on him, but sometimes it was a sweeter, more pungent scent and I knew that someone had thrown a half-finished joint into the overgrowth around the courts as soon as they'd seen me coming, and I'd pretend I didn't notice, because I wasn't out to bust kids for a bit of weed. I was there to confront them about bigger issues than that – about life.

Lil Smooth was standing at the edge of the court with his arms folded sullenly across his chest and an arrogant and sulky expression on his face. His eyebrows were furrowed together real right, so that his whole face seemed screwed up with the tattoos, like he was thinking about something really serious, or just mulling over something that made him mad.

I came to stand next to him and threw my glance out over the court where his eyes were watching the players run back and forth, too.

"You not in this game?"

"What's it to you?"

"It's just a question. Lil Smooth, right?"

"You been watching me?"

"Chill. It's the chain." I nodded towards the bulky gold-plated chain around his neck, which spelt out SMOOTH in chunky, garish letters.

"You don't need to know who I am." Smooth turned to look at me and there was fire in his eyes; a kind of hatred that took me back a bit, because I didn't even know this kid, so there was no reason for him to look at me that way. It was intense. "Don't think I don't know who you are," he continued defensively. "You're that cop that's always sniffing 'round."

"I'm not sniffing. I'm here to play ball. Just like you."

Smooth rolled his eyes. "Sure. Not out to bust anyone for smoking a bit of grass?"

"I got bigger fish to fry than some punks with a blunt. Don't you know the kind of things that go down here?"

"Sounds like you oughta be out there fighting crime, don't it?" Smooth challenged. "If there's so much bad shit going down, what you doing here? Ain't got time for ball."

"I always got time for ball."

I didn't even know where I was going with this conversation, but I didn't want to stop talking to this kid. He had that kind of raw anger in him that made alarm bells go off in my head. He reminded me of Leo in the way that he had that smart remark for everything you said, and that kind of sarcastic coldness to him, like you were wasting his time. Yeah, he reminded me of Leo, and Leo's attitude got him killed in the end.

The kids on the court finished their game and began to retreat. I bounced the tattered old ball in my hand against the concrete a couple of times and looked over at Smooth meaningfully. "So, you gonna show me what you got?"

It was a short and intense one-on-one. Smooth knew his way around a court and had a nice crossover, but nothing amazing. Another one who knew that passion was nothing without talent, so had just given up on having either. There was no sparkling NBA career ahead for Lil Smooth. No nothing.

The game came to an end and we were both a bit out of breath and the mistrust between us hadn't completely gone away, but at least some of the glare had faded from Smooth's eyes. He gave me a short, curt nod.

"Not bad for a cop."

"I've been playing since I was your age."

"In some fancy burb away from here, I guess?"

"What makes you say that?"

"The way you talk. The way you dress. I can tell you ain't from round here."

"That's where you're wrong. I was born on these streets. Grew up just over there." I pointed down the road. "I played on this court right here. When to Harold Washington High School. Went to juvy in this very community."

Smooth let out a short, bitter laugh. "How'd a kid from juvy end up turning sides? Can't have been much of a gang banger if you're riding with the law now."

"I wasn't the worst kid in the hood, that's for sure, but I've seen all it has to throw at you. It wasn't that long ago I was your age."

"Thanks for the history lesson. Why do you think I care?"

"You remind me of someone I used to know."

"You don't know nobody like me."

"Those smart ass comments will get you on the wrong side of someone one day."

"Yeah? So what? You're always gonna end up on someone's wrong side eventuall. Hanging with the wrong crew. Wrong place, wrong time. Wrong colours. Drive-by gone wrong. Might as well throw a little back out there."

"I used to think like that, too."

Smooth let out a long, bored groan and rolled his eyes again. "I don't care what you used to do at my age. Leave me alone, man. Arrest me or bounce."

"Anything I should be arresting you for, hey, Smooth?"

He let out a little laugh and gave another little sarcastic smile. "Of course not, Officer."

I raised my eyebrows – a little sign that I knew what he'd been smoking and the crowds he'd been running with. "Yeah. Thought not. Look, I got to go. Be safe, Smooth."

Basketball court in the hood. 2006. I was eighteen. Me, Winston and Leo were playing another game of ball. Out of all of us, Leo had probably had the most talent, but he cared the least, so it put us all at a pretty even level, which made for a fairly entertaining game.

"Hey, Reggie, how's your old man doing?" Winston threw out between shots.

"Same old. Looking for work. Job here and there. Sniffing around. Yours?"

"Factory gig for now. I was asking 'cause there's an opening down there. Thought your Dad might be interested."

"Maybe. I'll tell him to check it out."

"Will you two pack it in?" Leo groaned. "This is meant to be a ball game, not parents' evening. I don't give a damn what your daddies are doing. Let's play."

That was Leo. So angry. So sarcastic. I can't say I blamed him though. He had it the toughest out of all of us. A different home every other month. A whole bunch of people passing him around. At least me and Winston had family, even if we didn't get to see much of them.

We played the game for hours, until the sun began to set and the streetlights flickered on; dim and orange, making our shadows stretch across the courts. That's when we knew it was time to get moving, because it wouldn't be long before those courts became the scene of the underground economy.

We walked home together, laughing, joking, and stopping to take some munchies that weren't ours, and we sat down on Winston's front porch to smoke and chat until the early hours of the morning. Those were the good times – young and reckless and laughing. Long nights, just the three of us.

CHAPTER FIVE

Nowadays I live in a town just a short bus ride away from the hood. You might ask why I live outside my old hometown if I really care that much about turning the place around. Well, I've got kids now you see, and even though I was born and raised in the hood and turned out alright, I don't want my own kids torn between the decision of fitting in the hood and chasing a dream like their Daddy; because I know how easy it is to make the wrong choice.

We bought our house just a year ago. I never thought I'd have a mortgage and a house of my own. I always thought it was destiny that I'd live in some run-down rented shack of a place like I had done as a kid, and have too little time and too little energy to keep it clean, so that I'd spend my life in dust and squalor, cramped between four tiny walls.

Things didn't turn out that way, thank God. I live in a three-bedroomed detached place with a big front yard and a back garden where our dog and kids can play. Rosie keeps the place spick and span. She's my wife. We met back when I was still a rookie in the police force- barely in my blues. There had been a charity ball on to raise money for the force's chosen charity and Rosie had come along with her friend Bella, who'd been dating one of the guys on the force at the time.

The second I'd seen her my jaw had dropped. She was the most beautiful thing I'd ever seen and so different from the girls I'd grown up around. She just filled the room with her grace and elegance. She had been wearing a little black dress with sheer black tights and a cute pair of little heels and her long black hair had been partly up. I remember that it was her eyes that had caught my attention the most. They'd been large and dark and innocent, and when she'd glance my way, they'd sparkled with just a little mischief.

That was Rosie, though – elegant, but mischievous, too; the perfect mix of beauty and rebellion. She had that kind of spontaneity and thirst for adventure that had kept me going as a young boy in the hood, but she also had the refinement in her that I was seeking to create in myself. She was everything I wanted and wanted to be. Perfect.

She was studying her Bachelors in law back then. Now she's studying for a masters. That's my Rosie. Intelligent as she is beautiful. I loved and admired her from the very first day we met at that ball. I can't remember who asked who to dance first, or if we just kind of found each other on the dance floor, but I know that as soon as we started speaking, that was it. Love was happening.

Through my training and growth at the academy and through all the challenges I've faced in life since, Rosie has been my rock. My world. That's why I never expected her to come back with me to the hood. I wanted to provide her with a safe, secure life with everything she needed. I wanted my kids to be safe, too. So we lived our life just a bus ride away from the grim reality that had been my childhood and adolescence; close enough to return, but not close enough to get drawn in.

Our two kids were awesome little people – Kenya and Jordan. Kenya was five now and Jordan only three. It was hard to believe that I was somebody's father. I didn't feel old enough or smart enough to be responsible for the lives of a whole little family, but I was trying every day to be the man they needed me to be.

Leo looked worried and Winston and me knew that something was up. He'd been in even more of a bad mood than usual at the basketball court that morning, and lobbed the ball to the other side of the court when he missed a shot. Winston and me exchanged glances.

"What's with you, Leo?" I asked him. "Are you being moved again?"

He shot me an angry glare. "No. I ain't being moved."

"Then what?" Winston continued, having returned from picking up the ball that Leo had thrown away. "'Cause you've been in a shit mood all morning."

"Shannon called," Leo admitted. He sat down at the edge of the court and put his head in his hands. "She said she's pregnant. I'm only seventeen and I ain't got a job or apartment or nothing. How am I meant to look after a kid or do anything a guy's supposed do when your girl is prego?"

"I wouldn't even bother about none of that," Winston retorted. "Knowing Shannon, it ain't even yours."

"Shut the f...up!" Leo flared. "She wouldn't do that to me. The kid's mine. Did the dates. It makes sense."

"What you gonna do then, Leo?" I asked.

Leo shrugged. "Whatever I have to, I guess. I don't want my kid to be raised like me."

I gave him a brotherly slap on the back. "You'll figure it out, bro. You always do."

Rosie could see that I was dog tired from a day on the beat and she gave me a beer and came to wrap her arms around my neck and sidle up to me as I let my body relax into the sofa.

"Tough day, baby?"

"No tougher than usual. Same shit, different day. Got to testify in court next week. Jimmy Powell has got his trial."

"What you gonna say?"

"The facts, Rose. That's all I'm there for. I know he did it. But I also know why he did it. He's just another desperate kid stealing to try and fit in or try to get by. Let's just hope the judge goes easy on him, and if he ends up in the clink, that it does him the good it did me."

Rosie rolled her eyes. "Don't call it 'the clink', baby. That makes it sounds like you were in prison. A detention center isn't the same thing."

"Close enough, though, right? What is it, baby?" I teased, "You don't like the thought that you're shacked up with a convict? What would your daddy say if he knew?"

She gave me a playful shove. "What daddy don't know doesn't hurt him."

"He still just thinks I'm the hero cop, right? Boy from the hood done right?"

"That's right."

"Something else was bothering me today, too."

"What's that?"

"There's this kid hanging on the courts. Goes by 'Lil Smooth'."

"How original."

"You know how these kids are. Just looking for an identity."

"Go on. What's got you all troubled about this kid?"

"He reminds me of Leo."

Rosie's face creased with sympathy. She knew how things had gone down with Leo and how it had made me turn my life around and she laid her hand comfortingly on mine. "You think he's heading down that same path?"

"They all are, Rosie. That's what makes this job so damn hard. There's no way to reach all of them, and the cycle's never gonna stop until the hood is dead. That means education. It means funding. It means better supports. It means jobs and opportunities that inspire hope. Rehab. That town just needs the rest of the world to care about it. Then maybe some of the kids would turn out alright."

"I know it's tough to see them out there, baby, but you're doing all you can do."

"It don't feel like it sometimes. The system's screwed. I mean, nobody helps these kids when they're young and desperate. They're invisible. But you bet that when they do wrong, they're not invisible no more. Then the system sees them. They pay twice – once for being born in the hood, and once for giving into it."

"I think you blame 'the hood' too much for the choices those kids make. I mean, you and Winston turned out alright, and you grew up there."

"I was knocked straight, Rosie. Most kids' wake-up calls come too damn late."

Rosie took my drink out my hand and laid it down on the side. She turned my face towards her and gave me a kiss. "Don't think about it anymore, baby. Leave the streets out there. You're home now."

CHAPTER SIX

At Harold Washington High School again. Mr Branch had called me in. Once again, he greeted me with a clammy handshake and a friendly, nervous smile, and ushered me to sit down in his cramped office, overflowing with school reports and incident reports, but not a single college application form.

"Good to see you again, Mr Branch. What can I do for you?"

"Reggie, thanks for coming. I have a student I want to talk to you about."

I sat down on a chair with a broken spine and nodded. "Alright. What's the trouble? Dealing?"

"Yes, but it's more than that. I mean, which student here hasn't taken something or passed something on?"

"Alright. Then why did you call me in if you're not after a bust?"

"I thought you might have a personal interest in this boy."

"Why, is it someone I know?"

"Sort of. His name is Randall Harris."

I felt a lightbulb go off at the same time as a familiar tug pulled at my stomach. "Any relation to Leo?"

"His son."

Leo's son. I'd almost forgotten about the kid that Leo had had when he'd been barely more than a kid himself. I'd already been inside when the kid was born, and then Leo was killed before I got out, so what had happened to the child had been a mystery I'd never chased. I don't know why. Probably because I wondered what the kid of a friend I'd had a long time ago in a troubled time would ever want to have to do with a guy his criminal father used to roll with when he was young. I'd let the story of what happened to Leo's son remain untold. Until now.

I leaned forward with eager interest. A heavy guilt was beginning to gnaw away inside me, because I knew I hadn't done right by Leo's kid. I'd never looked in on him or made sure he was OK, like I should've done. Last I heard, Shannon had taken her kid and got out of town, and for me, that was as close to a happy ending as the kid could have gotten – away from the hood that had shot down his Dad.

"I didn't know Leo's kid went to this school. I thought he got out of town."

"He's come back," Mr Branch told me. "He's living with his grandmother now."

"What happened?"

Mr Branch sighed heavily, and sat back with his hands clasped in his lap. He shook his head woefully. "From what I understand, she just let herself go, and it just went from there. After Leo died, Shannon couldn't cope. She started drinking, but held it together a while. I think she still took care of Randall as best she could. Three months ago, her brother was shot. She started drinking heavier. Found out her liver was packing in. She got sick. Didn't stop drinking. Got sicker."

"She died?"

"She's still alive, but she thought it was best that Randall lived with his grandmother for a while. She needs to take care of herself before she can take care of a kid, and she knows that. For now, Randall's here at Washington."

"How old is he now?"

"Fifteen."

Fifteen years... And yet it seemed like yesterday. I could still remember so clearly the worry on Leo's face when he told me that he had got Shannon pregnant, and how he'd vowed to do whatever it took... He'd stood by that promise. He's stolen and dealt and fought until the bitter end to make sure there was food in their stomachs. God knows that before juvy, I'd have done the same in his shoes.

Yeah, I'd have thought that the only way to survive was to play rough. If only I could've told him back, then that there were other ways to get by. If only I could have told him that there was a light at the end of the tunnel if you could only hold on long enough.

Leo would have been a good cop, if he'd have had the mind to try. He could always tell when someone was bullshitting him, and he knew how to put pressure on someone to be straight with him. Who knows? Maybe me, Winston and Leo would have been the policing dream team – me, with my level-headedness and desire to just do some good; Winston, with his serious nature and attention to detail; and Leo with his ability to crack even the hardest nut. Yeah, I think we'd have been a good team – although none of us were rolling together any more. Life hadn't worked out quite like that.

"Tell me what's he's getting up to."

"He's at the start of a slippery slope," Mr Branch told me. "He started off selling dollar caps, and then went missing for three weeks. I've heard he's been seen around since, but apparently he's laying low. I reckon he's probably messed with someone he shouldn't have messed with."

"He's on the run?"

"Who knows? Whoever knows what the hell is going on with these kids."

So, Leo's son was heading down the same path as Leo. Dollar caps. Those were sleeping pills that the kids were using these days to get high. One or two made you drowsy, but three or four and the ability to push past the sleepiness gave you a super rush. Barely legal highs; the sort of thing we'd take a kid in for having, but would let go with a warning. But that's where it started. Yeah, it started with dollar caps, weed and molly, and ended up with a needle in your arm and dirty spoons.

I didn't know how I was going to help Randall, but I knew that I had to do something out of loyalty to Leo. Sure, it had been fifteen years since I'd last seen the friend I'd once known, but I still remembered the many times he'd got me out of a tough spot or had my back when I'd needed someone watching out for me. I still remembered painfully how hard his life had been, and how different it could have been if he'd had someone there to lead the way. I couldn't help Leo in time, but maybe I could still save his son.

CHAPTER SEVEN

I can't remember the last time I saw Winston. We hadn't fallen out, as such, but we had different priorities in life that kept us apart. Once, we'd both had the same dream – to make it as cops and then return to the hood to make it better. Except, once Winston had left the hood, he'd never found his way back. He said that things were worse there now than when we had been kids and that he'd done his time. He wanted to enjoy a more peaceful life and to leave the past behind. Me, on the other hand, I knew that the hood would keep getting worse until someone made it better; and I wanted to be that person.

Still, tonight, I knew I needed to talk to him. Randall was out there somewhere, in trouble, and probably making some, too, and two sets of eyes were better than one when it came to looking out for Leo's son. So, I gave Winston a call and told him to meet me at the bar on Delton Street, where we'd used to buy drinks even though we were underage and holler at girls in their mini-skirts.

Winston was waiting for me when I arrived and he looked pretty good, I guess, but different from how I remember him when we were young. He'd lost that edge that made a hood kid stand out. He'd smoothed out those rough edges now, combed his hair and wore a white collared shirt even off duty. He looked healthy, well and rested, like someone with a normal life should.

"Winston," I called, as I got close, "how's it going?"

He stood up with a grin and held out his hand to shake mine. "Good to see you, Reg. It's been too long."

"Way too long."

I sat down at a booth with Winston and looked him over again. He was dark-skinned, like me, and had cut his hair close to his head. I still remembered it when it was a mass of wild curls that no comb could tame. But then again, once I'd shaved patterns into my hair and worn gold pendants and stolen kicks, so I guess we'd both changed since then. He was wearing a white shirt with the top button undone and a pair of dark denim jeans. His sleeves were rolled up to the elbow so that I could see the three black dots tattooed on his lower right forearm. I remembered putting them there myself with a needle and the ink from inside a ballpoint pen. I had the same one, and so had Leo. It represented us – a trio. It was faded now.

Winston gestured for a waitress to come over and ordered us both a drink, and then it was down to business.

"I came here with something important to tell you."

Winston didn't look surprised. "I guessed you had something you wanted to say. After all this time, I didn't think this was a social get together."

"Hear me out, Winston. It's about Leo's son."

I saw Winston's eyebrows shoot up and he let out a long breath and ran his finger around the rim of his glass with that familiar serious expression on his face. "Yeah, that's right. I remember that he had a kid. Boy, wasn't it? Randall."

"That's right. He's fifteen now."

"If he's anything like his Dad, then I'm guessing you're here 'cause he's in trouble?"

"Mr Branch called me in. Apparently he's gone missing. He was selling dollar caps –"

"– who isn't?"

"And then he disappeared. Branch is thinking that he's running with a bad crowd and he's pissed someone off."

"Well, one thing I remember about Leo is that he always knew how to piss someone off."

"I feel like we gotta do something."

"Like what?"

"Look out for him. Make sure he's doesn't get his nut busted. Make sure he don't go the same way as Leo."

Winston looked down at his glass with a sad expression and sighed heavily. "He was too young to die like that, and you know he was only doing all that shit to look out for his kid."

"Yeah, he was a good guy under all that sarcasm and anger."

"He was. And you know, he loved that girl too. What was her name?"

"Shannon."

"Yeah. He loved her. They were real good together. I even thought that maybe she'd be the one to change him. I thought he might get himself sorted. For a while, he seemed like he was on the right path."

"I remember. When she was six months he was telling us that he was going straight and gonna get a job as a car salesman, remember?"

Winston let out a throaty chuckle. "Like Leo would be able to sell a car! He couldn't get on with nobody, and you need to schmooze in a job like that."

"He was convinced he'd be a natural and making the big money."

"Until he realised that nobody was gonna hire him."

"Then he went back to the only life he knew."

We both shook our heads. It was a sad story, but not a new one. So many ghetto kids try to turn it around and fall flat on their asses. In fact, it happens so often that hardly any make the effort to even try anymore – they've all seen someone they know dare to dream and come crashing down. Leo was a shining example of an epic fall from grace – a three-month determination to succeed, followed by a shoot-out and early death when he got desperate and real life hit home.

"So what happened to his Momma?"

"Drinking problem."

"Dead?"

"No. Just trying to get Randall away from her while she self-destructs."

Winston nodded and shook his head again. "At least she had the sense to get him out the way before she lets it all fall to pieces."

"That's more than some do."

"So where is he now?"

"He was staying with his grandmother until he went MIA."

"I got ya, Reggie. I'll keep my nose to the ground for him."

"Does that mean I'm gonna see you back at 33 Division?"

Winston smirked. "You know I transferred for a reason."

"Yeah, you didn't want to run your beat in our old hood."

"I'm over it, man. It brings back too many bad memories and there's too big a chance that I'm gonna end up shot up by some meth-head. I wanna go home at night, you know? I've got a wife and kid that depend on me."

"Me, too, but it's about more than just us. You know that."

"Sure, sure, I do, but I've done my years on 33 Division. I tried and saw my fair share of kids getting shot and druggies having seizures and choking to death. I've waded through all that shit and seen the people die in all the ways that you can in the ghetto, but I ain't seen one thing I do make a difference. You nick one dealer and there's three more to take his place. You put one violent kid behind bars and his old gang goes looking for someone to blame, and it starts another war. It's thankless work that does no good, Reg. I'm better off just doing a normal, dull nine-to-five in a safer community. I get to go home every day to my wife and read my kids their bedtime story. And that's all I want for life. I'm not after glory. I don't want to be a hero. I'm not like you, Reggie."

"I'm not trying to be a hero," I retorted. "I'm just trying to be loyal to the place I grew up."

"Why? It weren't loyal to you. It chewed you up and spat you back out."

"Someone's gotta do something, or the next set of kids and the next and the next will all be faced with the same life. Nothing will change if someone don't do something."

"I agree with ya, Reggie. I just don't think the work we do makes the difference you think it does – but good on you if you want to try. I'm rooting for ya, Reggie, I am, but it just ain't for me no more."

I sighed. I was disappointed that Winston had let go of our dream so easily, but I couldn't say that I didn't understand why he'd want to walk away. When you had a family, they came first.

"How's Elizabeth doing?"

Elizabeth was Winston's wife; a white woman he'd met about five years back in a supermarket buying groceries. I never thought that Winston would be one to live the middle-class life with a white woman in a nice community, but I was happy for him. Elizabeth made him happy and he loved her. Their kids were happy and had everything they needed. Winston had it all and he was holding onto it with both hands. I couldn't blame him for that.

But still, it amazed me how much we'd both changed. It wasn't so long ago – not really – when we were both up to our necks in a mess of our own making.

CHAPTER EIGHT

The heist had been my idea. I was tired of pulling the same old tricks stealing shit worth chump change from the same old stores, and Leo had a baby on the way. It was time to change our tactics. It was time to do something big. I was the master of theft; I'd never been caught. So why should I keep setting my sights so small? It was time to play in the big leagues.

My idea was to pull a robbery on the factory where Winston's Dad had been working. They'd just cut him loose because they'd lost a big client and orders were down – and it wasn't fair. The man was a hard and honest worker, but had lost his job again. But I was going to make it right. That factory had tons of expensive equipment and cash boxes to rob. My idea was to go and take as much as we could and for once have some money in our pockets for a while.

The factory was a bit sketchy. I knew from Winston's Dad that they paid their workers in cash for some unscrupulous tax reason, and that meant that on payday – Thursday – there was always a ton of cash inside. Today was Wednesday.

"Look guys, here's what we do," I told Winston and Leo as we huddled together in our booth at the bar on Dalton. I looked around furtively to make sure that nobody was listening and leaned in even closer. "We go down to the factory early tomorrow – before the workers get in. We'll have to time it right. We want there to be as few people inside as possible. Just the managers, and the cleaners maybe. We'll break in through the back door."

"And then what, genius?" Winston asked sarcastically. "A fifteen, sixteen and seventeen-year-old with no weapons demand the cash and they just hand it over to us? They'll knock us on our asses and we'll go straight to jail."

"We'll have weapons." It was Leo who spoke, quietly and secretly. He lowered his voice until it was so much of a whisper that we could barely hear it over the sound of the drunks and the jingle of the vending machines.

"What? You got a weapon?" I mocked. I expected him to say no, but Leo instead smirked and raised his eyebrows.

"I got a piece we could use."

"Where you got that from?"

"It don't matter. I got it. Would that do?"

"It's a gun. That's all we need."

"So what?" Winston asked. "We go in there with a gun and demand the cash. That's it?"

"That's it," I replied confidently. "We tell them all to get down on the ground and ask for the cash. We'll have to wear ski masks, of course. We don't want them to see it. But otherwise, it's as simple as."

"I don't think it'll be that easy."

"Grow a pair!" I scoffed. "You've heard Damien's crew boasting about all the burglaries they've pulled, and they're all as thick as two bricks. If they can get away with it, then we can."

"I'm game," Leo nodded. "I got to get some money together somehow. Let's do it."

"Yeah, come on, Winston. It'll be easy."

"Easy for you to say!" Winston retorted. "You're fifteen, Reggie. You'll get a slap on the wrist if you get caught."

"You're only sixteen, Wins. You wouldn't get much more. Come on. You got this."

Winston sighed heavily, but the pressure of not wanting to appear the wimp got to him and he shrugged. "Fine. I'm in. But none of these pantyhose over our heads kinda thing. If I'm wearing a mask it better be one that actually hides my face."

"I've got some old beanie caps," I said. "We'll cut come holes out for eyes and pull them down. Nobody will know who we are."

"Let's do it," Leo grinned.

So it was decided; simple as that. At the crack of dawn the next day, we gathered in the alley behind the factory, with a bag for our cash and a gun shoved down the back of Leo's pants. Even then I felt a little thrill in what we were doing, but it didn't feel like crime; it felt like justice- getting what was mine, what I deserved.

"Here, give me the gun," I urged Leo.

"What? Do you know how to shoot?"

"What do I need to know how to shoot for?" I argued. "I ain't gonna shoot no-one. I just need to wave it around a bit."

"First rule of guns is that you don't hold one unless you're prepared to shoot it."

I rolled my eyes. "Look, you guys both said it – I'm the youngest. I'll get off the lightest. So I should hold the gun. What can they do to you guys then? Breaking and entering?"

"I don't think it works like that, bro," Winston said. "I think we're accomplices to armed robbery, even if we don't have guns in our own hands."

"Whatever. Look, the sun is coming up. Let's get on with this."

I could see the factory ahead and it looked quiet. There was no movement behind the windows, because the workers were out. I was expecting nothing more than the owner or manager counting their money in the office on the second story, and maybe a couple of cleaners milling around, but apart from that, a clean sweep.

Time to get real now. No speaking as we made our entry. I put a finger to my lips and jerked my head towards the back door of the factory to let them know it was time to go. We crouched down low like ninjas, dressed all in black, and pulled our masks down over our faces as we moved. It got hot quickly inside that makeshift mask and I could feel the wool fibres tickling my throat, but I was determined not to cough and give the game away too soon. I didn't want anyone to see the gun until we were inside. I had to limit the witnesses.

Once inside, the scene was exactly what I thought it would be. A single cleaner was half-heartedly pushing around a mop, and the only other person inside was a slim, official looking white guy holding a bunch of papers. I pointed the gun straight at him and thought it was kinda funny the way it made him throw his arms up in the air, causing his papers to fly loose and float down to the ground. I did a visual sweep of the premises to see what there was to take.

"This equipment is too big to carry," I said out loud. "Let's stick with the cash." I pointed the gun threateningly at the manager. "Where is it?"

He pointed a quivering finger up the stairs to where an office stood with glass windows overlooking the factory floor. I gestured that Winston and Leo should go ahead and get the cash, while I barked orders at the owner and cleaner to get down on the ground. "Stay still and no-one gets hurt."

Moments later they returned with the cash, and we began to walk backwards out of the factory. I kept that gun pointed at the two witnesses until the very last second. And then that was it. Out scott free. I began laughing as we raced away down the alley, as far and fast as we could go; exhilarated.

"Woooo!" I whooped as I ran. I could hear Leo laughing behind me and even Winston shouting, 'Oh man! Oh man!'.

It felt like a victory as soon as we were out of the factory and even more so as we got further and further away. I pulled off my mask as soon as I was out of the alley as I didn't want to look suspicious with my face covered, and Winston and Leo did the same.

"I told you guys! I told you guys!" I celebrated gleefully. "In and out. Just like I said."

"Yeah, you told us!" Leo grinned. "How much d'you think we got away with?"

"Who knows, man, who knows! The important thing is that we got away."

"I couldn't believe the way you held that gun like that. So cool, man."

"It was pretty cool," Winston agreed begrudgingly.

We all raced towards my house because my parents were both out and we gathered in the living room, drawing the curtains tightly closed so that nobody could see us. Then we poured out the cash on the ground and stared at the pile of green, wide-eyed.

"Woah. That's a lot," Winston breathed, his eyes as round as saucers and bulging with excitement.

"Yup. That's a lot," I said.

Leo began to count a wad of cash, and then I started counting, then Winston, too. For a bunch of kids who'd always flunked math, we were suddenly full-on accountants when it came to working out the dough we'd got away with. In total, $3,614.

"Ah man, ah man – that's like a grand each!" Leo said. "That's gonna make Shannon happy."

"What are you gonna tell her?" Winston asked.

"I'll think of something," Leo shrugged. "Maybe I had a grandpa die or something. Got me some inheritance. Or maybe I'll just tell her what she don't know won't hurt her. She's not gonna turn it down. She ain't got nobody else to pay for her and that baby. She knows I'm only doing what I gotta do."

"So, you're spending it on the baby," I said. "Winston, what are you spending it on?"

"I don't know, man, I've never had that much cash. Maybe I'll just hold onto it for now. What about you?"

"I'm gonna get my Mom a washing machine and tell her that a friend gave it to me 'cause they were evicted. I'm sick of seeing her wash the clothes in the tub, or drag that trash bag of laundry late at night to the laundromat. You know what goes down there."

"Same thing that goes down everywhere around here."

"I can't believe we got away with it!" Leo said gleefully. "Oh man, that was something, hey?"

"Yeah… that was something."

If what had happened next hadn't happened next, we probably would have all gone and spent that money the way we'd planned and gone on believing that we'd pulled the perfect crime and got away with it. Perhaps one successful heist would have led to another, until we were addicted to the thrill of a .22 and a list of demands. Perhaps we'd have gone from a factory, to a jewellery store to a bank and thought we were pretty hot stuff; never getting caught. Except, you always get caught. If you keep on going, you always get caught. And for us, we'd already pushed our luck too far.

We were fools. I'd thought that if I could get away with stealing smokes from the store, that armed robbery would be no different – a walk in the park. Except, that the police don't care about a missing pack of smokes, but they care a lot about three men with a gun on the loose. That's why they went asking questions. That's how they heard from someone down at the bar that they'd overheard three kids they knew planning a job. That's how they got us.

It was just gone two in the morning when the squad cars surrounded us. I saw the lights flashing through the blinds before I heard the door being kicked in. Leo and Winston were still with me. We'd fallen asleep eventually, giddy from excitement and dreaming sweet dreams about living the high life with our ill-gained riches.

The police had surrounded us and knocked down the door. Winston didn't run. He knew the gig was up and that only the guilty run away. So he just held out his wrists and let the cops take him. Leo had them chase him a while around the bedroom, but two cops cornered him and got him in the end. Me, though, I didn't want to be caught, because my parents were in now and I didn't want them to see me arrested like that.

So, I ran. I ran like hell. What else did you expect me to do? I was fifteen and scared. I thought I'd get sent down for a long time. I thought I'd get shot to death by the police in my own home, like I'd heard had happened before. I thought it was all over, and I was ready for that.

I made them chase me almost three miles. I ran like a panther through those streets and all the hookers and dealers that I'd given warning to before did the same for me and pointed me this way and that away from the police, but I could only run so far. I was caught eventually, and taken down hard; slammed against the hood of a squad car and cuffed with my hands behind my back.

It was so fun, then. Not so cool. I wasn't thinking about how much of a legend I'd be in the hood for getting picked up by the police or how much street cred I'd get for this, because there was no glory in getting caught. The street cred came with being above the law; invincible. Now I was just another crook, on his way to jail and not Yale. Not special. Not talented. Just a kid who got caught.

CHAPTER NINE

I roamed the streets that night looking for Randall. Somewhere out there was a kid on the run, and I knew what it felt like to be that kid. How many times had I had Leo's back when he'd rubbed someone up the wrong way and then all three of us had had to find someplace to lay low until the storm blew over? And who knew what underground dealings Randall was involved in – there were all kinds in the ghetto. A crime for every flavour of criminal.

Maybe he'd borrowed some dime caps and promised to pay back double. Maybe he'd fallen short. Maybe he'd got into a fight when high and drew the blood of the wrong guy. Maybe he'd done something real stupid this time.

The first place I went was to the basketball courts – because that's where I always went when I was sniffing someone out. Don, Kye and Tre were out shooting hoops. These three kids were your low-level kind of trouble, but not bad kids really. They smoked things they shouldn't smoke, and drank when they were underage, but we'd all been young once… They weren't violent, and although they might fight back if someone threw a punch, they weren't out to cause trouble. They just wanted to play ball.

"Hey, D!" I called, and gestured for the leader of the crew to come over. He was about seventeen himself, with cornrows in his hair and a black sports jacket slung over his shoulders. He walked with an attitude, with a bit of swagger, but he was always cool when I asked him wuz up? He seemed to be one of the few kids round here who recognised the good I was trying to do.

"Heeeyyy," he drawled, long and slow, "wassup, Reggie?"

"I'm looking for someone."

Don held up his hands disinterestedly. "You know I ain't no snitch, man. Snitches don't get no bitches up in this hood. Don't know that I can help ya."

"Relax, D, I'm not here to make a bust. Just looking out for a kid. He's the son of a friend that I'm just trying to do right by. Been missing."

"Aw, man, that's tough news. You don't want no missing kid round these parts. Never good news."

"Don't I know it. I think he's on the run. Maybe got himself into a bit of trouble. Now I'm not trying to make no arrest, y'hear me? I'm just trying to get him home safe. No priors. The kid still stands a chance."

Don pursed his lips together and rolled his tongue around inside his mouth for a long time, like he was thinking, and eventually he nodded and gestured his boys to join the conversation. "Reggie's looking for a missing kid. Might be in trouble. Listen up and see if you can help the man."

I smiled gratefully for his help. "His name is Randall Harris. He's fifteen. Black. Deals dollar caps, from what I hear. Lives not far from here, on Jackson Street."

"A fifteen-year-old black kid that deals? Nah, don't know nobody like that," Tre replied sarcastically. "Come on, officer, you gotta give us something to go on here. This is the 'hood, you know. At least tell us who he rolls with."

I pulled out my little pad to look at the notes I'd taken down when Mr Branch had gone into detail about Randall and all he'd been getting up to lately. "He hangs with Dre, Tyrell and Matt from what I hear."

"Aw yeah, I know Tyrell. Don't know the name of the kids he hangs with though," Tre piped up. "He's had a couple of newbies hanging on his heels lately, looking for a bit of adventure and a way to earn some dollar."

"Where's their spot?"

"Here, there, everywhere," Tre told me. "They hang out a lot by Cook's Place, in the car park at the back."

"Right." I wrote down what he was saying. "What else can you give me?"

"Not much. Like I said, don't really know 'em."

I thanked the boys for their time and headed straight for Cook's Place which was a diner a few blocks over. Me, Winston and Leo had spent a fair bit of time there when we were young. It was the sort of place that just kept going forever. I'm pretty sure that some of the waitresses had been working there since I was a kid, but at least the owners were loyal to their staff, which was more than could be said for some.

I didn't recognise the teen hanging out by the dumpsters in the lot behind the diner, but I imagined that he was Tyrell. I flashed my badge at him as I approached and held my hands up to calm him down when he began to reel off a list of reasons why I couldn't arrest him.

"Cool it. I'm not looking for you. I'm after a kid named Randall. You know him?"

Tyrell, who was tall and lanky with old faded acne scars on his face and a spider tattoo behind his ear shook his head. "Don't know nobody by that name."

"Are you sure?" I asked meaningfully, "'Cause I ain't got a reason to take you in right now, but I could find one."

"Seriously, man. I don't know no Randall. You got the wrong guy."

"You better not be lying to me. I got your number, kid."

"I'm telling the truth."

I narrowed my eyes suspiciously and fixed the kid with my best cop stare, long and hard, hoping that it would make him break, but he stayed cool as anything, so it almost made me believe him. I pointed a warning finger in his direction. "If I find out you roll with him and you ain't told me where he is, then I'm coming for you, Tyrell. And oh, by the way – stop slinging dollar caps. Don't think you can't get busted for a 'legal high'. You're making kids act crazy, and if one of them shoots another, and those red pills are to blame, I'm gonna track down the one who put that stuff in their hand."

Tyrell scowled but gave a little nod. I doubted that he was going to stop dealing a damn thing, but hey, maybe he'd find some other way to waste his time.

I chased down one lead after another all night, until it was getting real late, and I knew I had to get home. Just one last call to make.

Randall's grandma, Flo, lived in one of the poorest parts of the hood in a little apartment that could barely be called more than a hut, made out of drywall and some sort of aluminium, it seemed. At her age, she'd given up on trying to keep a lawn and had had the whole thing paved, so that it looked grey and dreary like a prison. She kept some old mutt hound tied up to a post by her chair when she sat in, rocking on the porch; it watched over her and barked loudly at every passer-by to warn them to stay away. I quietened it with a piece of jerky from my pocket and greeted Flo with a kindly squeeze of her shoulder.

"Mrs Lawrence, nice to see you again."

"I told you, Reggie – call me Flo. Now, tell me, you found my grandson?"

"No luck, I'm afraid. I've been pounding the pavements all night long, but nobody knows where he's got to."

Flo began to breathe hard, and the sound was strange and lisping emanating from behind her loose dentures. It made the sound echo around her mouth like there was a tiny audience inside giving a tired round of applause. Her black hair was now mostly grey and tied back in a loose bun, but still her bald patches showed through the loose strands. She was wearing a faded floral dress and long grey stockings. She looked like an old ma'am from a Western movie or some 'gater hunter's wife from down in the swamps.

"That boy'll be the death of me," Flo muttered, shaking her head. "At first it was his mother, getting pregnant at her age – but

I understood, I was her age once, and it happened to me. Then she started dating that boy Leo, who got her in no end of trouble and it did him in, in the end. Now their kid has gone off the rails too. What's a woman gotta do to have a relative who'll just sit down and shoot the breeze without looking to get themselves up to no good?"

"I hear ya, Flo, I hear ya. But you know as well as me what these kids are up against out here. They're not looking to cause trouble, just looking to fit in."

"It would be nice if you could get 'em away from the bad crowds, but if you're stuck in the hood, you're stuck, and all you got is the hope that they'll listen to what you got to say and try to let some of the sense sink into their thick skulls. Never have any luck there, though. Kids! They always think they know better. Think they'll find some glory in dealing or shooting some place up, no matter how much you tell 'em that a quiet life is what they need. Nobody wants a quiet life at that age. They're all looking for something 'more'. They think they've found it when they get accepted into some gang and it's all fresh and exciting and dangerous – until someone gets shot, or locked away or stabbed, and then real life hits home."

"Well, all we can do is try and get to them before it gets taken too far," I said wisely. "That's what I'm here for. It's what we're trying to do."

"I just don't know where he'd go," Flo sighed irritably. "It's not like I know the boy all that well. His Momma took him off when he was just a littl'un and didn't get in touch with me again until she needed someone to look after him again. Last month was the first time I'd seen him since he was a babe in arms, so how am I meant to know what's going on inside his head?"

"How are any of us meant to know?" I sighed. "My guess is that he was feeling unsettled and outta sorts after coming here and has done something stupid in an attempt to fit in. Maybe he's taken on more than he can chew and got himself in a tough spot. Or, maybe he's just fed up with his Momma and this hood and decided he wants to try it out there on his own. Who can say? Look, I'm sorry that I haven't got better news for you today, but I swear that I'll keep on looking out for him. Just give me a holla if you hear anything, or see him, alright?"

"Will do, Reggie. I'll keep praying that he shows up alive. Maybe his Momma will sort herself and come back with somewhere better to take him."

"Let's hope."

CHAPTER TEN

That night I couldn't relax; couldn't shake the feeling that I was missing something, and it must have showed on my face, because Rosie came to sit beside me and looked at me knowingly with those big brown eyes of hers.

"What is it now, Reg?"

"It's Randall."

Rosie's eyes softened and she sighed. She looked at me with affection and understanding, and patted my knee. "Baby, you've just gotta think of him as any other kid you look out for."

"He's not just any other kid though, is he?"

"No, he's not," Rosie agreed. "But if you let yourself think too hard about Leo, then you're gonna lose your focus. Just use your logic, like you would with any other case."

"I don't work cases, Rose. I'm not a detective. I just follow orders, or go out on the beat and step in where it's needed. I'm no detective."

"No, but you've got something even more useful."

"Oh yeah?"

"Yeah. You've got shared experience. You've been where that kid is. Maybe that'll help you get inside his head."

"You're right about that, Rosie. I was just like him once. Maybe that's why it's so hard to get him out of my head. And there's so much guilt over what happened to Leo."

"What happened to Leo wasn't your fault."

"Maybe I didn't pull the trigger, but I put him in the firing line."

"You were a young, dumb kid."

"Is that an excuse?"

"It's a reason. And who says you're trying to excuse anything? You're the first one to own up to the mistakes you've made, and if you don't think there's some kind of redemption in the work you do, then what's the point? You're doing good out there, babe."

"Not enough good. Not fast enough. Geez, Rosie, I look at what the hood's become and it makes me feel like I'm never gonna meet nothing but dead ends. It was bad when we were kids, and I think it's even worse now. It's like I can't turn a corner without seeing a gun, or a drug deal going down, or some stupid kid doing some senseless violent thing just to prove he's got what it takes."

"That's just why that place needs people like you, Reggie. If you get through to just one kid who would've ended up dead or on the inside, then it's all been worth it. If you can prevent just one Leo."

Leo didn't die the night of the robbery, or any time that soon after, but that doesn't mean that the robbery wasn't the root of all the events that led up to his death. He died in prison. Some brawl that got out of control. From what I heard, Leo started it with his big mouth. You see, it's all well and good mouthing off when you've got a crew behind your back to jump in when that kind of stupidity causes a riot, but it's a whole other ball game when you're on your own in the lion's den.

Who knew what stupid and trivial thing had caused Leo to go off on one. All we really know is that he crossed the wrong guy, a fight broke out, and Leo ended up dead in the prison yard. He wasn't even eighteen.

I heard about it through my Mom when she came to visit with tears in her eyes. I know it broke her heart that Leo – who had been in and out of our home since we were just young kids – was dead. I know it broke her heart thinking about that little baby left without a daddy and another young girl left alone. And, I knew it scared her, because I was on the inside too, and I could just as easily be stabbed or strangled or beaten to death over some little thing gone wild, because beasts get vicious inside cages.

It rattled me when I heard the news, and made me think, hard, about my life choices. Me and Leo had always followed the same path. Always. Same school. Same interests. Same mistakes. Same girls sometimes. All our lives our little gang of three had mirrored each other's idiocy and recklessness and we'd all ended up behind bars, except, now Leo was dead, and it was time to stop doing everything together.

I didn't want to die, and I didn't want to be in prison either. Honestly, when you're living on the kinds of streets that I grew up on, you can't help but get caught up in the drama and thrill of the them vs us mentality of down-and-out kids against the police. It gives energy to a tired old dump to glorify the chase of blue lights and sirens on your tail. Except, it stops being fun when you're caught. You realise it's not a game, because once those bars are drawn shut, you can't choose to opt out. You're there, for as long as they command, and you've got nothing but time to think about your life.

When I was in juvy, I did think. A lot. I thought about how all my life I'd done the easy thing. The quick fix. I earned cheap respect from reckless people by doing stupid things, instead of working on building my own self-respect by rising above the squalor and violence of my community. I bought into the myths of the hood, which told me that there is glory in taking a life or losing one; like the battles we fought out there as kids on the street were epic stories that would go on when we were going; like Vikings conquering ground.

The truth is, nobody knew who we were. The rivalries that got blood spilt were as small as the little run-down and forgotten hoods where they played out. Lives were lost for the sake of the pride of a handful of young men who clung onto it for dear life, because pride was all they had. Yet, as important as our pride or our glory or the concept of 'respect' was to us back then – we were small, and we were insignificant, and the world hadn't even heard of us, let alone would it remember us when we threw our lives away on petty street conflicts. The world stayed away from us, because the world knew better to engage in such violence and depravity. Yet, we let ourselves get sucked in by it all and fooled ourselves into thinking that we were warriors in a glorious and timeless fight. Timeless, yes. But glorious? No. No more glorious than a murder, or rape or gunfight in any part of the world in any other time. We liked to think of ourselves as heroes, defying a law that was out to get us, and rejecting a system that wasn't on our side. But we weren't heroes. We were rebels at best and criminals at worst.

I was a criminal now. There it was on pen and paper; signed and sealed by court records. Thank God for my young age. That was the only reason I could claw back some opportunities and turn my life around. It wasn't too late. It's never too late.

I changed my mind then about who I wanted to be, and I made the choice that I was going to be my own man, with my own mind, and that I would decide for myself what was glorious or worth respect. No longer would I find my glory in the gutters or feel like I deserved respect for taking from others what I couldn't earn myself. No. I was going to live a real life full of real achievements and real connections to people. I was going to live with real purpose. Enough of the lies the ghetto tells us, that we've been forgotten and we don't matter. I was going to make them remember. I was gonna do something to make me matter.

CHAPTER ELEVEN

I'd never visited Leo's grave. Not once. Maybe it's because of the guilt I'd always felt over being the one to get Leo put in that prison, which would be his last home. Or maybe it was because it filled me with dread and this kind of heavy sickness to think that if I'd have been a little more like Leo, or maybe just a year or two older so that I'd ended up doing adult time, that I'd have been the one six feet under. Or maybe it was just because as much as I wanted to hold onto memories that gave me a cause, I also wanted to forget that once I was someone capable of such recklessness; that I'd once hurt people and stolen from them, fought, lied and cheated, like people didn't matter.

Yet, here I was now, standing at the foot of Leo's grave. It was clear that nobody visited here often. Sitting in a cemetery with a thousand other dead bodies, Leo's headstone was cold and cheap, with his name etched into the rough stone angrily and sharp. The grass that covered him was overgrown and tangled and weeds had sprung up.

This cemetery made me feel a deep and wrenching sorrow; not just for Leo, but for the circumstances of all our lives. Sixty percent of the graves counted out the dates of lives that had been too short. I'd walked around, working out all those ages. So many dead young men. Some black, some brown, some white; all victims of poverty and pride.

I walked through that overgrown cemetery for hours, examining all the dead and feeling that emptiness inside when I thought about

what a waste it all was. Gregory Payne, Billy Thor, Darnell Jackson...
I didn't know who these people were; but I bet you anything they
died for the 'honour' of their name.

And there was Leo. Yup, another guy who'd thought a cheap
insult was worth the insult he threw back, and worth the self-made
dagger that somebody had dug into his side. The inability to back
down from a fight had caused this all, and it happened time and
time again.

"Hey, Leo," I said softly. I stood at the end of the grave and
sighed heavily. The smell of the earth was pungent and sweet. It was
a humid today with clouds gathering overhead. "I thought I'd come
visit you. Or maybe I was just looking for your kid. He's a lot like
you, Leo. A big-mouthed banger who doesn't know when to quit.
I hope you're looking out for him up there, my brother, or else he's
gonna be joining you before too long."

"Wow. You know how to honour the dead."

The voice came from behind me, and it was slow and sarcastic. I
turned to see Winston standing behind me and I half-smiled, turning
back to look at the grave.

"What you doing here, Winston?"

"I don't know, Reg. I don't know. Maybe the same thing you're
doing. Coming to remember the things I need to remember, and let
go of the things I should forget. Looking for a troubled kid who's
too much like his father."

"Then yeah, we're here for the same reason."

Winston came and stood beside me with his hands buried deep
into his pockets. He was frowning so deeply that it caused wrinkles
to appear around his lips, making him look sterner than ever and
morbid. He kept sighing these big, heavy sighs that made his whole
chest rise and fall.

"Such a waste, ain't it, Reg?"

"Yeah, Winston. It is. What d'you think he would've done if he
hadn't ended up here?"

Winston chuckled bitterly. "Ah, Reg, he was always gonna end
up here. You and me both know that. Remember how me and you

used to talk sometimes when we let the act drop, about how we'd like to turn it all around someday and get away from the hood? Leo never joined in those conversations. This place was in his blood. He loved being in a place where being wild was a good thing; where a smart mouth gained you cred. Could you ever imagine someone like Leo on the force?"

I laughed to think of it. "No. He'd be out on his ear in a week."

"Improper use of a weapon?" Winston guessed.

"Yup. He'd probably be out shooting at birds on the highway when he was meant to be busting a drug deal."

"Or using the drugs he was meant to be busting."

We both laughed. We were both cops now, but once Leo had been our brother, and he had been every bit as much trouble as the guys we busted daily out there now. It was strange to think how much people could change.

"I still miss the guy," I sighed.

"Me too," Winston said. "He was crazy, but he was our crazy. I know you feel guilty over what happened to Leo, Reg, but he would never have stopped like we did. He'd have never stopped."

"We'd have never stopped if we hadn't got busted."

"Then maybe in some screwed-up way it was for the best. At least two of us turned our lives around. If we hadn't have been stopped, then we'd have carried on down that road forever." Winston shuddered. "It terrifies me to think about it now. I got family now, you know? I coulda given all that up to rob and fight my whole life. So easily."

"I know what you mean," I nodded. "When I think about when I first met Rosie... I was dressed up in my blues. Respectable. Do you think a girl like that would ever have fallen for some back-street thug with blood on his hands? And then the kids came along... Such good kids, Winston. They've never done no wrong. They won't even skip out on a piece of homework, let alone be taking drugs or causing trouble. Makes me wonder how kids like that could ever come from me."

"We've all got it in us, Reggie – to be better. Every one of us. It's just when you're young and all you can see is the filth and mayhem around you, you don't dare dream that big."

"Have you had any luck tracking down Randall?"

"'Course I haven't. Don't you remember how Leo used to give us the run-around when he got in trouble?"

"Yeah. He'd lay low for days just so nobody would come after us to get to him."

"He got us into a hella load of trouble, but he did a lotta things to have our backs too."

"Ya fool," I scolded the ground where Leo lie. "You had to go in there with your big mouth again. And now we're here missing ya, bud." I turned back to Winston. "I guess I kind hoped I'd find Randall here, visiting his Dad."

"Our Leo was hardly his Dad," Winston sighed. "In prison and dead before he even knew the boy. If I was Randall, I'd be real mad at him."

"He should be mad at me," I replied. "It was my fault."

"We all chose to go along with it that day."

"But it was my idea, and I convinced everyone to do it. And for what? Some quick cash."

"You wanted to buy your mom a dishwasher, wasn't it?"

"A washing machine."

Winston smiled, almost like the memory was a fond one. "It's hard to believe those kids were us. Y'know, I thought about blaming you back then, Reg. I did. But I knew that you made the suggestion because you were struggling with life, and we went along with it 'cause we were too. We can go on and on about whose idea it was on that one day, but we'd built a life around being trouble, so if we hadn't got busted on that day, it would've been another. At least getting busted put us on a different path. I don't blame ya, Reg. And I know Leo wouldn't either."

"But what about Randall, hey? There's a kid out there somewhere in trouble with no father to set him on the straight and narrow."

That made Winston laugh out loud. "You know as well as me that Leo woulda been out there selling dime caps with him. Let's not make our Leo out to be no angel. He was trouble through and through, but a good guy all the same. Funny, how people can be both."

"All good intentions, all stupid ideas."

"That's right, my friend. That's right."

CHAPTER TWELVE

I wasn't on the beat, but I was roaming anyhow. Maybe I'd run into some kids I'd run into before and could ask them about whether they'd seen Randall. Maybe I would just get some time to clear my head. My mind had been running like crazy since seeing Winston again at the cemetery. Standing there, me, him, and Leo in his grave, had brought back a lot of memories from when us three used to roll together. It hurt me a bit to know how much had changed. Me and Winston weren't so close anymore, and Leo was never gonna roll with anyone again. Then, on the other hand, I was glad in a strange way that it wasn't like that anymore, because I'd changed. Winston had changed. Two of us had moved on and one of has had passed on, so nothing could be the same as it was.

I'd spent most of the evening strolling around the same parts of town that I usually did – the bars and the basketball court, and I'd run into a few familiar faces, but nobody had any news that was any good to me. So, then I decided to walk down by the river.

I had memories there, too. When me, Winston and Leo had been much younger – before the teenage angst and mayhem, before the crime and fast thrills – we'd spent our time getting silly at the river, rolling and splashing in water that was more slime and litter than river; but we were used to the rougher things. We'd hung out for hours, eating PB and Js and slurping down sodas. We'd chat about school and who was getting into what kinda trouble, and life hadn't quite hit us yet. The days at the river came before the times where hard choices had to be made about running with a crowd, or breaking free and running ahead. You know, the thing is, when you're running ahead, sometimes it feels like you're being chased. We all feel safer in a crowd.

It was dark now. Not quite pitch black, but a very heavy twilight; just dark enough to feel dangerous. The river was stagnant. The water was a muddy brown which began to look black as the night set in, and was covered in a green scum and floating tin cans. Had it always looked like that? Had we really swum in that garbage? Funny, they were good memories. If there had been scum and garbage, those memories hadn't stuck – only the way we used to laugh and feel hopeful when we were young.

I was coming up to the bridge. There had been a railway over that bridge once, until that line was cut off. Now it was just broken tracks and a bridge that nobody ever climbed, apart from the odd jumper wishing to float amongst the tins after life got way too much.

There was a figure up ahead standing under that bridge wearing a hooded jumper and smoking a cigarette; alone. It made me suspicious. There was probably a deal gonna go down soon. It was the perfect place from it, away from the crowds and hidden from view. I didn't break my stride; I wasn't out to bust anyone tonight, but maybe seeing my face would make a kid think twice before dealing something they shouldn't.

As I got closer and my eyes attuned to the shadows, I realised that I recognised the figure under the bridge. His heavy bling was glinting in the moonlight. Lil Smooth.

"Hey Smooth, what you doing out here on your own so late? Better not be slinging out here."

"I ain't in the game no more," Smooth replied, his voice husky and tormented. He took one last deep drag on his cigarette and threw the butt to the ground, stomping out the embers with the heel of a tattered sneaker.

"I wouldn't admit to a cop that I ever was, if I was smart."

Smooth gave a small, low chuckle. "Like you don't already know who's slinging."

"I turn a blind eye occasionally – if it's for the larger good."

"Oh yeah? What's the line, Reg?"

"The line?"

"How do you know if it's for the better?"

"I like to think some kids doing nothing more than slinging the low-class stuff might still have a chance to turn it around. Anyway, I got bigger fish to fry."

"I hear you're looking for Leo's son. I hear he was your old partner."

"Oh yeah? And where'd you hear that?"

"Around."

"Uh-huh. You know anything about that?"

Smooth smiled a small, knowing smile, and rolled his tongue around inside his mouth like he was chewing on a secret. "A kid should know better than to tell a cop if he's in the game."

I smiled. "They call you Lil Smooth 'cause you're a smooth talker?"

"Something like that."

"You know, it's not safe out here at this time of night. Not out here in the dark. Anything could go down."

"In these parts, it goes down anywhere – don't matter where the lights are. Nah, Reg, I feel safer here, where fewer people are passing. Standing here under this bridge, I get a good look at them before they figure out who I am. Gives me chance to take my leave if I need to."

"Are you in trouble, Smooth?"

"Who in this place ain't?"

"I can help you with that."

Smooth laughed. "I doubt it."

"Why's that?"

"I heard you used to be trouble once."

"You heard right."

"You think you're able to save the rest of us just because you got clean? Not all of us are so lucky."

"I know that. I know I got lucky," I answered quickly. "But you know what, some of us have luck come to us by chance, and some of us have got to make our own. I didn't plan to get lucky, but since I did, I'm gonna do what I can to make others make the right choices, and turn back while they still can."

"My dad lived and died out on these streets and his dad and his dad… we're like part of this place. Rooted. I don't belong nowhere else."

"You know what, Smooth? Maybe you don't belong somewhere else, but that ain't necessarily a bad thing. If all the good ones leave, the place just gets worse and worse. Some of us have got to stay."

"So you're saying I should turn it all around and then sweep in like Superman, just like good old hero Reggie?"

"Something like that, Smooth. Yeah. Something like that."

Smooth shook his head dolefully. "No, Reg. If I ever get out of here, you'd never see me again."

"Well, that'd make me happy, too. As long as you were doing OK somewhere."

Smooth gave me one last, long look and shook his head with a sigh, like I'd disappointed him somehow. "I gotta bounce, Reg. Good luck with finding Randall. I hear he's pretty good at hiding in plain sight."

CHAPTER THIRTEEN

The call came out over the radio just a little after eleven pm when I was cruising in the patrol car with my current partner, JJ. The static, urgent voice over the stereo told us that there had been a shooting on the corner of 52nd and Howard. Just another night in the hood.

The victim was a young black male. The shooter was on the run. The helicopters had been sent out to scour the streets for the gunman, but any kid who grew up in those streets knew just where to hide in her many dark corners. We could hear the rotor spinning from where we were on the ground; the swift *vvt vvt vvt* of the blades turning created an urgent soundtrack to our arrival. Sirens other than ours were already blaring.

I looked over just in time to see a stretcher being loaded into the back of an ambulance, although I didn't catch sight of the victim. Then I saw Winston, attending a scene outside his patrol, and immediately I knew.

"That's Randall on that stretcher, isn't it?"

"The EMTs say he's gonna make it."

"We can only hope. Where's he been hit?"

"Left shoulder. Gone right through, but doesn't seem to have hit any of the major organs. Just trying to stem the bleeding. If they can get it under control, then it should be just a stitch-up job, as long as no sepsis sets in."

"Let's thank God for that. I'm going to go see him."

I stepped away from my partner and raced to the back of the ambulance, where the EMTs were still trying to patch up the kid inside. When I finally got close enough to see the face of the victim, my face creased in confusion.

"Lil Smooth?"

He looked up at me and in his eyes, amongst the pain and that tough-nut act he was trying desperately not to break, was a little spark of amusement. "Hey, Reggie. Guess who?"

"It was you the whole time. You knew I was looking for you and you didn't tell me who you were?"

"That's not the point of laying low, man. Besides, you ain't my friend."

With that, the EMTs gently instructed me to move aside and shut those doors. Astounded, I watched the ambulance drive away with my friend's son, and his last words to me were so cold. I stood staring after that ambulance for a full minute or more in numb silence before Winston came and brought me back to the world with a slap on the back.

"A drink, Reggie. Come on."

We ended up in the same old dive bar we always did, nursing our scotch, and while I wallowed in despair, Winston seemed to see some sort of comic irony in it all.

"That's Leo's son, alright."

"It's not funny, Winston. He could've died tonight."

"But he didn't. He had a close call – and you and me both know the good that one of those can do. It's a wake-up call. Let's hope it knocks him straight."

"It didn't have to have happened," I sighed, taking another gulp of the bitter spirit in front of me. "I saw him. Just last night under the bridge I was speaking to him. Had no idea who he was, can you believe it? What kind of friend am I? Been so distant from Leo's kid that I didn't even recognise him standing right in front of me."

"You're too hard on yourself, Reg. What were you ever gonna do? Raise the kid? There was nothing you could do. We were still kids when we got out of the joint; just like Leo was when he knocked that girl up. None of us were ready for that kind of responsibility. She took off with him, and for all we knew, Randall was safe and living well. We weren't to know."

"But we should've known, Winston. If we'd have taken an interest, we'd have known."

"We had to make our own paths. It was time. Leo didn't have to die in that place, but he chose to make a scene, just like he always did. He decided to raise his voice and square up, instead of think twice and back down. We ain't gotta be sorry for that. We were inside too, and we didn't make the choice to go down in flames like he did. Ending up in prison was on all of us, but ending up dead was on Leo. He had no self-control. We weren't responsible for him dying, and we weren't responsible for looking out for his kid."

"How can you say that, Winston?" I asked in disbelief. "We were brothers for life. We were family. That means Randall was ours to look out for too. We shoulda watched out for him."

Winston let out a low and derisive snort. "Are you still buying into all that shit, Reg? Ain't what you trying to teach the kids out there nowadays that any guy who leads you down a bad path ain't no friend? We call each other 'family' and then we're willing to go to any length to protect each other. We'll bleed for each other. We'll die for each other. But at the end of the day, all we're doing is holding each other back from the people we could be if we weren't born to believe that our only place in the world was having someone else's back. So, what if you'd have watched out for Randall? What would you have done, Reg? Taken a bullet for him? Lied for him? Broken the rules for him? Because he was *family*?"

"The loyalty people have for each other out there is the only good thing in this whole damn place."

"It's not loyalty, Reg. It's fear. Fear of being alone in the wild. Fear of being the weakling. Fear of being the prey. Being a father has taught me a thing or two about loyalty. When my son was growing up, do you think I was teaching him how to make a fist and which guns you could hide in your pants the easiest? No way. I was teaching him how to respect people and make his own way. To educate himself. To aspire. My loyalty to him was making sacrifices, working overtime, parents' evenings – because I wanted better for him. Ghetto loyalty isn't trying to make someone else's life better; it's trying to keep them there on your side, right down in the gutter with you."

"He was just a kid. He *is* just a kid He's not learned those lessons yet."

"Y'think? Well, he got shot tonight. Seems like someone's loyalty turned sour."

"We coulda been role models to him."

"Yeah, I guess. But you forget, Reg. We're not the good guys in their eyes no more. We're the enemy. The blues. Out to bust them and put them away. Randall was never gonna trust you. You'd never have filled the hole that Leo left."

"If I'd have just recognised him, Winston, I coulda pulled him off the streets last night and away from that trigger."

"And he'd have been back out there again some other night, causing trouble again." Winston chugged back his drink and laid it flat on the table. He looked at me with a hard and cynical stare. "Learning the hard way is the only way to learn out here, Reg. No tough-love speech – no matter how passionate or real – is gonna get through the skull of some knucklehead who's convinced that street cred is going to be the cornerstone he builds his life on. But a bullet might get through to him. It just might."

I didn't know what to say. Winston was being cold; so cold to the son of our fallen friend. But then, I kind of understood what he was saying, because we'd both lived the tale ourselves. When we were kids, we'd been preached at by do-gooders and the reformed criminals, and we just believed they'd gone soft. They couldn't steal from us the glory we saw out there in the rebellion and rivalry. They couldn't convince us the thrill wasn't worth chasing. They couldn't convince us that the small change we got our hands on through theft and deceit was nothing compared to what could be ours if we took the long, hard route to income. They tried to tell us, but we wouldn't listen.

Maybe Winston was right. Maybe nothing would have been different, even if I'd been a friend to Randall from day one. Maybe Leo and this neighbourhood was just too much in his blood from the start. Maybe it was always destined to end this way. And maybe, just maybe, the same hope existed for Randall that had been ours – the possibility that he could still save himself. The small chance that a close-call might be the only voice he'd hear.

CHAPTER FOURTEEN

Seeing him under the harsh glare of hospital lights, I finally noticed the resemblance to a ghost of the past. The same long nose and hard eyes. The same little upwards turn at the corner of his lips that made it look like he was always smirking or about to come out with something sharp. In Randall now, I could see Leo.

It almost made me take a step back, because it was hard to confront the past that way. What shocked me most, perhaps, was the anger that was still seething in Randall's eyes, like I'd let him down. Or maybe it was just anger in general. I sat down on the cheap seat at his bedside.

"So, you couldn't stay low forever, huh?"

Randall rolled his eyes. "I ain't talking."

"What, you don't want to snitch on the guys who shot you? They don't deserve your protection."

"But I deserved to get shot, Reg. As mad as it seems out there, there are rules. If you break one, they're gonna get ya, and you can't complain it ain't fair, 'cause you knew what the consequences would be."

"If you give me names, details, your story... I can get them arrested and charged. You'll be safer with them behind bars."

That made Randall laugh out loud. "Really, Reg? I thought you only preached redemption. Willing to put some guys behind bars, just for little ol' me? And just because you and my Dad rolled together once."

I looked down at the ground and sighed, then back up at Randall. "You knew the whole time, and you never said a word."

"There was nothing to say."

"You're right. I did used to roll with your Dad once. He was a good guy."

"He was a fool who got locked up."

"Says the fool who got shot."

"What you tryna say, Reg?"

"I'm trying to say that you're a lot more like him than you know, and that bad things tend to happen to reckless guys. You need to slow it down a little, Randall; take a step back, and think about the choices you're making."

Randall rolled his eyes. "You think I ain't heard that all before – from the teachers, from my Grandma; geez, from my mom once before she lost her mind? It means nothing."

"I heard about your Mom. I'm sorry she had issues. And I'm sorry I wasn't there."

Another roll of those dark, angry eyes. "You think I care about that? I don't even know you, man. And I didn't know my Dad. Why on earth would I feel like some guy that used to hang with the Dad I never knew outta be in my life? You're a strange one, Reg. Real odd."

"What's odd about it? You know, I used to live by those same rules that you're talking about. Back in my day, if you rolled with someone, you were family, and you looked out for one another. You're Leo's son – that means you're family."

"But you don't live by those rules no more. They don't go with the rules of the rest of the world – the law."

"You're right. They don't go."

"You dropped your line of questioning real fast," Randall pointed out. "Are you here to interrogate me or reminisce about my old man?"

I gave a little half smile. Randall knew why I was here. "I was just checking in on a friend's son. Someone from my team will be here later to take your statement. Be careful, Smooth."

CHAPTER FIFTEEN

Rosie and me sat together on our bed. I was trying to act normal, because God knows my wife put up with a lot of low moods from me, and I didn't want to put any more on her, but good old Rosie always knew when something was on my mind, and she always tried to get inside my head, so that she could go through it with me and help me bear the load.

"Randall's going to live, baby," she soothed. "So there's nothing left to worry about."

"It's not whether he lives or dies this time, Rose," I tried to explain. "It's whether he gets the message and makes a change so that there is no next time."

"You know yourself that there's only so much you can do, Reg. These kids aren't really kids. They're young men, and they have to make their own calls."

"I feel responsible for him. Imagine if it was one of our kids sitting in a hospital with a bullet through their shoulder. Would we tell ourselves then that there's only 'so much we can do'? This is what my job is becoming, Rosie. Just giving up on kids time and time again, because there's only 'so much I can do'. God damn it! I need to do more."

"And what is 'more', Reg?" Rosie asked. "You can't raise them. You can't take them off the streets. You can't watch every single one of them every minute of the day. You can't undo the things they've seen and done. All you can do is try your best to convince them that there's a better way, and help them there if you can. But, at the end of the day, you can't force them to change their lives. They've all got parents and teachers and other people around them. Why do you feel like you're the one responsible?"

"I remember what it was like," I sighed. "You didn't grow up here, Rosie. You don't know. You don't know what it's like to be raised by parents who ain't got the time to steer you right because they're out working double shifts to pay for the clothes on your back. They have to choose between being there to keep you steady, or feeding you. And then most of these kids have a whole load of other problems they gotta face – family in prison, peer pressure, drugs, gang culture, poverty, abuse. Their parents are struggling, the schools are struggling, and the whole world turns their back, because with tough cases like these, *there's only so much we can do*. Sometime, someone's gotta do more than so much. They gotta to do something."

Rosie smiled at me tenderly, but I could see that she still didn't entirely understand, and why would she? She was raised somewhere safe with her parents around and well-off, and well-funded schools. She'd been sheltered, and that meant she believed the best in people. But the truth was, in this place, no kid was going to make the right choice off his own back, because his values were so tied up in hood rules that there seemed no other way.

"I just wish there was something I could do that would make the real difference that I'm trying to make."

"You're someone who wants what's best for these kids, and will fight in their corner to the end. That's more than many have. That's worth something."

"I'm also the one who's gotta bust them when they take things too far, and nine times out of ten, they're just dumb kids who started off slinging dollar caps and then moved up to weed and then something else and something else; not realising the damage their actions could do, and then suddenly finding themselves in too deep, and in debt to too many people so we gotta step up because they're becoming the bad guys. But inside their heads, they're still running that same old high-school logic that told them selling dollar caps was a good idea to raise some cash on the side."

"Even that's doing good, baby. Every time you put someone away, you stop them selling something that might send someone else into a bad spin, and, at the same time, you give them a wake-up call which might help them change their lives."

"You see, that's the story I've been telling myself, too, Rosie, but I'm starting to wonder if it's true. I mean, if I take one kid slinging drugs off the streets, you know that the next day there's gonna be another kid stepping straight up to take his place. The first kid might be off the street, but the drugs never are. The drugs always find a way. Then that kid you put in prison? Yeah, if he's smart, he'll realise that he's heading down a bad road and turn it around. If he's dumb, then he'll end up listening to the stories that all the hard-core dealers, gang bangers and murderers have to tell on the inside, and maybe he'll get this sick idea that there's some glory in that kind of living. Then, when he gets released, he's more dangerous than he was before he went inside."

I sighed and put my head in my hands. Rosie came and wrapped her arm around my shoulders, kissing my temple sweetly. "You're doing good, baby. I promise you, you're doing good."

"Am I, Rosie? Sometimes I start to lose faith in it all. Sometimes I think that seeing one more kid give up on himself and shoot or get shot... I might just give up on it altogether."

"And if you did, it would be no crime, Reggie. If you did, then you'd get more time with your own kids, and you can put all that loyalty and compassion into raising them. Two great kids are still an achievement, even if you can't save them all."

"But then I'd be another one just walking away, wouldn't I? And every time one of us does that, we're giving all those kids with a chip on their shoulder another reason to believe the system don't care. 'Cause too many of us are walking away. Someone's gotta make the streets their problem. Someone's gotta tough it out until it changes. I used to think I was the one who was gonna do that, but there are days, Rosie, when I just don't think I got it in me no more. I never see the change I'm trying to make. Only the damage that those boys do to themselves every day. And I'm the one they blame. They always think I'm out to get them, but I'm just tryna give them the chance the streets don't give 'em."

Another day, another beat. I headed first to the basketball court and checked in on the boys. Who were all there, shooting hoops. It was just gone one pm. Some of them should have been in school, but here they were as usual, bouncing rubber against the concrete.

In the past, I'd always noticed their absences from school, but it hadn't bothered me. I mean, at least they were playing ball instead of dealing drugs. But today... today it did bother me, because these kids weren't doing a damn thing to change their circumstances and I knew for a fact that they'd go on and on about how the system had failed them – when they hadn't bothered to show up.

Then I'd feel guilt for feeling that way, because I remembered what it was like to be in school at that age. There was so much disruption and petty crime taking place behind those doors that you were lucky if you learned anything at all. The kids who kept their heads down often had the worst time of anybody, and most of the teachers were worn out from trying to break through to kids who had already given up.

You see, for these kids to get anywhere in life, it takes effort on both sides. The system needed to buck up, invest in these kids' futures and never stop trying to find new ways to make a difference and tackle the real and pressing issues in the kids' lives. On the other hand, the kids had to help themselves. When a teacher planned a good class, the kids needed to show up and be engaged. When a team of volunteers raised funds to create apprenticeships and skills training, the kids needed to take hold of the opportunities others had worked to give them.

Today, I said nothing. I didn't even stop for a friendly chat. What was the point? I could spin them a story about how an education would one day get them far, and they might even pretend to be inspired because they liked me, but, tomorrow, they'd be here again, playing ball. So, I walked on.

On the corner of 52nd and Howard, I saw a drug deal going down between two teens with furtive glances. I could bust them, and give them both records that would follow them for a long time and affect their job prospects and learning opportunities, or I could turn a blind eye and let them both get blazed so that they wouldn't bother chasing an opportunity anyway. I walked on.

Outside the drug store, a homeless man rambled nonsense, chugging from a cheap beer can and shaking his hat at passers-by for change. People ignored his grubby presence and his blatant alcoholism. I, also, walked on.

As I passed the salon, I looked in and saw Mrs Peterson getting her hair bleached another shade of blonde, while a cigarette dangled out her mouth. Her twelve-year-old son, Jay, had been in trouble multiple times for missing school. Childrens services had been called in because his clothes and shoes were falling apart, and he didn't seem to be getting enough to eat. The social services was meant to cover his keep, but there Mrs Peterson was, spending the money for her kids on cigarettes and hair dye. Unfortunately, spending your kid's money on cheap pleasures wasn't a crime I could arrest her for. So, I walked on.

And as I walked on, and on, and on, I began to feel that heavy despair settle over my shoulders once more, because what Rosie said was right. There was only so much you could do, and what little you did was not enough.

And somewhere out there, Randall was still caught up in this endless cycle of disappointment and drudgery, making bad choices, and watching others do the same. But what could I do? What can anyone do?

CHAPTER SIXTEEN

I answered my cell and recognised the voice on the other end of the line. It was Mr Branch. He sounded cheerful and bright, but I wasn't feeling so optimistic these days.

"Reggie!" he greeted brightly. "It's been hard to get hold of you lately."

"There's a lot of work to be done out here."

"Oh sure, I bet. Still, I was hoping you might have some time to come down and do another one of your assemblies?"

I let out a short chuckle. "Really? I didn't think you'd want me back after what happened to Randall."

"What's Randall got to do with it?"

"He was there in that last assembly I did, wasn't he? Obviously it didn't change a thing."

"Ninety-nine percent of the time the things we say will fall on deaf ears. But we do it for the one percent, and so that none of those kids can ever say that we didn't try. Besides, I think it means more coming from you than any of us. You're a good role model for these kids."

"Any more of a good role model than a teacher? Those kids just don't have any respect for authority. And when I was their age, neither did I."

"You're not yourself, Reg. Is this all over what happened to Randall?"

"He's Leo's son. It shouldn't have happened the way it did."

Mr Branch sighed down the line. "Come down to the school when you finish your shift, Reggie. Let's talk."

I didn't know what I was doing here. There was nothing to be said, but Mr Branch wanted to speak anyway. When I arrived, he called me into his office, made some coffee, and sat me down.

"I'll admit, Mr Branch, I'm not really sure what I'm doing here."

"How many times do I have to tell you to call me Sean?" he replied. "We're both adults now." He sat back in his chair and looked back over me as though he were still seeing me as I was, a long time ago. "I still remember how you were when you were Randall's age. I remember the three of you – Leo and Winston, too."

"Trouble, huh?"

"Certainly not the worst I've had, but not going anywhere fast, either."

"I feel like you're trying to make a point, Sean. But I'll admit that I don't get what it is."

"I get the feeling, Reggie, that you're feeling hopeless. You're feeling like the cycle just goes on and on. And I get it. I really do. Do you think it's easy to be an educator in these parts?" He took a swig of coffee like it was whiskey, and rubbed his watery eyes with the back of his hand. He looked tired. His clothes were worn. His skin was weathered. His hair was thin. Maybe in another area, he'd have been a respected academic. Not here, though. Not here.

"Let me tell you about despair, six years ago, I had three-hundred and forty-one new kids join grade 6. This year, there are only fifty-two left in grade 12. That's two-hundred and eighty-nine kids lost to the wind in those six years. Now, don't get me wrong. Maybe some of them are out there doing some good. Maybe some are working, or taking care of their families. But a lot of them just gave up, or made a mistake big enough to put them off track forever. Unplanned pregnancies, drug issues, gang culture, juvy, or they just plain dropped out. Of the fifty-two that made it this far, only twelve have a grade C average. There is only a handful that might have the grades to make it to college, and, even if they get those grades, who's to say they'll have the funds?"

"Every day, I walk into a school where most of the kids won't make it, either because there's too much going on in their lives, or because they just don't care. They'll argue with me, and fight with me. They'll bring drugs and weapons into my establishment. They'll swear at me and spit at me, and act like I'm the devil because I try to enforce some order here. You'll try to encourage them, and when that doesn't work, you'll try to discipline them, and when that doesn't work, you'll just try to keep them alive to senior year."

"A lot of the time, their parents are too busy. You notice that parents' evenings are in thin attendance around here. Mostly because the parents are out working hard. Sometimes it's because they don't see the pay off in education."

"The kids haven't even reached eighteen and they're tired. They're worn out. They don't want to do it anymore. They don't see the point. And you see the despair in *their* eyes, and you've got to try and make them feel hopeful, even when you know they're probably not going to make it either."

"But, every now and then, a kid you don't expect pulls through. They turn it around. They put their head down. They do good. And then it's worth it. Those rare miracles are proof that the system can work. It just takes *more*. More dedication, more perseverance, more creativity, more compassion. Of the ones that do make it-there is one thing they have in common, they have a caring adult. These kids are very talented."

"Look, Reggie, what I'm trying to say - from one person trying to save those kids to another – is that we all feel like we're banging our heads against a brick wall sometimes. We feel like the system is broken and that we're just spinning cogs in a machine that's been broken for a long time. But... well, there is no 'but', Reggie. Our jobs suck sometimes, but somebody's gotta do it, or else the chaos takes over and nobody gets a chance to make it out alive."

CHAPTER SEVENTEEN

'd walked past the basketball courts – where the boys were playing hooky as usual – and then I walked on through downtown, and finally popped my head in at the pool hall to check no deals were going down in the men's bathrooms.

Walking in the door, I immediately stopped when I recognised the young man shooting pool on his own at a far table. It had been almost a month since I'd last seen Lil Smooth. After our last meeting, I'd backed off a little, because I thought maybe time would allow him to reflect a little on his actions. I thought maybe time was what he needed to calm down and see the error of his ways.

When he looked up at me and I saw the anger flash in his eyes, I knew that wasn't true.

"What you doing here, Reg?" he snapped. "Checking up on me again?"

"Just checking in, in general. A lot of stuff goes down here."

"Don't I know it."

"You should be in class."

"I should be a lotta things."

"Hey, cut it out, Randall. Enough of those smart ass lines. I'm tryna talk to ya."

Randall scowled at me and thrust his cue forward at the table, making a ball swirl into the corner pocket, clicking against others and sending them sprawling across the green. I took a step closer.

"How's the shoulder?"

"I'm playing pool, ain't I?"

"So it's healing good?"

"Yeah. It's fine."

"You're not laying low anymore."

"I paid for what I did."

"I still don't know exactly what that was."

"You don't need to know."

"Drugs?"

Randall gave me a warning glare and took another shot.

"You know, I've been where you been. I used to get in trouble once."

"So you keep saying. Again and again. Don't you know that no-one cares, Reg?" He circled the table slowly, like a shark. "You know, just because you were one of us – once – don't mean you *are* us. Your life and your problems were your life and your problems. This is my life, and I got my own problems. You think it helps me to know that you were me once? It don't."

"Fine, I get it. You don't want to talk about me. So, let's talk about you."

"What about me?"

"What's going on with you? Why are you out dealing and skipping school, instead of trying to get outta here?"

"There is no way out," Randall retorted, throwing me a resentful glare. "I ain't gonna be a cop, Reg. I ain't gonna be no scholar. There's nothing out there for me."

"That's a lie the world lets you believe."

"It's the truth. I've seen it. Time and time again."

"It's the truth because you *choose* it. It's the truth for anyone who chooses that truth. You can choose another way."

"What way? Taking a crappy job at the liquor store, watching my back every night in case someone pulls a gun on me, just so I can hold my head high and say I'm making an honest living? Yeah, there may be some working-class glory in holding down some shit job and making shit money, just because you can say you took the high road and kept the law, but that's not how I want to live."

"So it's make it big, or not make it at all? Is that what you're saying, Randall? If you can't be a big shot, you're not even gonna try?" His attitude made me angry, because it was how places like the ghetto stayed as it was. Everybody wanted to feel like they were important, and if they felt like a dazzling career in the NBA or some other glamorous field was out of their reach, then they sought the other kind of glory – out on the streets. Nobody wanted to feel invisible, so if they couldn't feel pride in a minimum-wage job, they'd find it in gang culture. "Not everybody gets to make it large. Some people are just going to be pretty ordinary, but there's nothing wrong with that."

"Ain't there? Sounds pretty shit to me."

"Only 'cause you don't understand what really matters in life," I retorted. "You ain't never had the love of a good woman, or the pride that comes with being a father. You've never seen your own name on a mortgage, or on a pay check. Those little – and ordinary – things, are small miracles that let you keep your head high. They're foundations to build your life on. They let you stand tall, because you *earned* them."

"I ain't gonna spend my whole life sweating and slaving under someone else's command for an average, dull, boring life where I can't even afford a new car if I want one, or to go out, if I want to. It's just not for me, and you ain't gonna convince me otherwise."

"So you'd rather spend your life getting shot at and hiding under bridges, then settle into something too ordinary? You're just like your father."

That made Randall mad. He threw down his cue so hard against the floor that it bounced back up again before cracking against the stool. He strode up to me and squared up like he was getting ready for a fight. His face was growing wrinkled with anger and his teeth were gritted.

"Just like him, am I? And how would I know? He's dead, and from what I hear – you had a lot to do with that."

I bowed my head and felt an old shame, an old guilt, rise up in me. I nodded. "Yeah, Smooth, you're right. I had a part to play in that. But so did he. Because, like you, he didn't know how to back down. He didn't know when to stop. He thought a smartass answer was worth whatever consequence that came from it. He was reckless. He hated the idea of being ordinary. Well, let me tell you something, kid – there's nothing more ordinary than another kid dead in a ghetto shootout. It happens every day to kids more interesting and more special than you. You're fighting an empty cause. You're putting everything you are into things that don't matter. You're gonna waste your life fighting other people's battles out of loyalty, and getting blood spilt for the sake of pride."

"Don't you dare lecture me!" Randall seethed furiously. "You had to get busted before you turned it around. I've been in your assemblies. I've heard your story. Don't act high and mighty. If you hadn't got caught, you'd have gone down the same path as my Dad. You'd have been dead out on the streets someday, too."

"And don't I know it. Don't I thank God every day that I was knocked straight. Don't I count my blessings that I met my wife, and had my kids, and have more love and purpose in my life than ever before. I had to be humbled before I made a change. I hoped that what happened to you would be your turning point. But you're not making that choice – to change. You're choosing to go right back to square one. Why, Randall... *why?*"

"Because it's all I know."

I sat with Flo on her front porch sipping tea from a chipped fake china mug. She listened to my story and pursed her lips, rocking back and forth in her chair. She sighed and shook her head.

"That boy of mine. Don't know what I'm gonna do with him."

"How's he been, since he's been back?"

"Oh, you know my Grandson. He's been moping around, acting like that stupid alter ego of his. What is it again? Groove?"

"Smooth."

"Ah yes. *Smooth*. Bloody ridiculous. He used to be a nice boy, but I blame his mother for that."

"How's she doing?"

"God knows. She never talks to me no more."

"I thought she was meant to be making a change."

"Maybe she is. Maybe she's passed out on a pile of needles. Who's to know?"

"You've given up on her."

"For a long time, I tried. But, there's only so much you can do."

There it was again; that phrase I hated. That little mantra of defeat that everybody was so eager to spread. Only so much. Only so much. Only so much. Flo had given up on her daughter – and what had happened? She'd let her addictions spiral out of control to the point that she was no longer fit to mother her son. Then *he'd* got himself into trouble, and convinced himself that that's just how life was. And so the cycle went on.

"Maybe you should reach out to her. Maybe she just needs a little help."

"God knows she's had my help. When she was young, I tried grounding her and keeping her all holed up, away from all the bad influences in the world. At first she obeyed, but hated me for it. And then she just began to sneak out. Then she got pregnant. God knows I wasn't happy about that, but I'm her mother, so I supported her through it. I scrimped and saved my hard earned cash to buy baby clothes and diapers and prepared myself to do it all over again – to raise another kid. And then her boy gets locked up. And then he gets killed. And she takes off. Doesn't tell me where she's going, of course."

Flo let out a long, sad sigh and shook her head. When she looked up at me again, I could see the pain in her eyes. "That hurts, you know. After all I did for that girl, she vanishes without a thought for her mother. Leaves me worrying and weeping every night. I called the police and they didn't know where she'd gone. A new mum with a young baby on her hip – vanished. It was at least a year before she called me, and by then, she was off the wagon. Had already started drinking, but I did my best."

"She'd moved a ways away, but again, I saved and scrimped for the fare, and went to see her as often as I could. I told her that if she wanted, she could move in with me and I'd help her raise that baby. But she said to me, 'No Mom, there's too many bad memories in that place. I ain't raising my baby there'. And I thought maybe there was something to that. But then it all comes back to the hood, don't it? And here Randall is, starting the whole bloody thing all over again. Maybe he'll knock a girl up and then get himself thrown in jail. Maybe he'll be the one shot and killed. I don't know what to expect, Reg, but I don't feel good about the future."

I reached out and held her hand for comfort. "You've got me looking out for him now, too."

Flo smiled a wrinkly smile and patted the back of my hand. "And I'm glad for that. But we both know that these kids are gonna do what they want to do, no matter how much we try and shake some sense into them. They've got to decide for themselves, otherwise we're just the monsters trying to control them. Because what do we know, huh? We just 'don't understand'. But I understand – sure I do. If I wasn't affected by my environment, then I wouldn't smoke twelve cigs a day. I wouldn't have partied all my youth instead of studying. I wouldn't have had my girl at sixteen. But you grow, and with God's help, you learn. And, if you can learn first enough, you can still make something of your life. However small, however ordinary."

"But these kids don't want ordinary."

"Of course they don't. Nobody wants to be ordinary. But that's when you learn to cherish the small things, like your baby's first steps or painting the porch. When you love the small things, they don't feel so small no more."

I smiled, because Flo was like me. She'd once bought into the fantasy that drugs and music and rivalry made the world go round; made life real – but then she'd learned that being another kid gone off the rails was about as ordinary as it gets, and chose to find joy in the small things, so that life seemed worthwhile.

I felt sorry for her that her daughter had cut her off time and time again, and that her grandson was making her sick with worry. She'd tried hard to do right by them, but, as I was starting to learn the hard way – *there is only so much we can do.*

CHAPTER EIGHTEEN

After years of little contact, it seemed like suddenly me and Winston were spending a lot of time together. Once again, we were at the bar, and, once again, I found myself drinking. I was drinking more and more lately.

"You know, Randall blames me for Leo's death," I told Winston matter of factly. "I tried to turn it around on him, to make out like Leo's death was down to bad choices, because I want Randall to make a change. But, really, I've always felt like I was to blame."

"And I've told you before, Reg, that it wasn't your fault."

"It was. And you know what? I'd got to a point in my life where I felt like I was coming to terms with that. Yeah, I may have pushed Leo into a place where his smart mouth got him killed, but I'd learned from that. I felt like I would find my redemption in going back to that place and making it better – to honour Leo. But, you know what? I'm changing nothing."

I took a huge swig of whiskey and wiped my mouth with the back of my hand. I sat back with my legs spread, and arms laid out. Completely done with even trying to sit upright and look the part of the good cop.

Winston watched me unwind, sighed heavily and then shrugged. "Well, you know what, Reg? Maybe you're right. Maybe it's time to give up on the old hood. I did, and I never looked back. Getting out isn't an escape if you keep going back. Looks to me like you're done with that place. You need to escape, once and for all."

"You know I can't do that, Winston."

"Why not? Why can't you do that? You've done your time. You deserve the kinda life you've worked for. Get away with Rosie and the kids. Join another station in a better area where all you gotta deal with is speeding tickets and littering. You don't need to put up with this shit no more. Let it go, Reg."

"Someone's gotta set that place straight. Someone's gotta do that job."

"And someone will. Why's it gotta be you?"

I sighed heavily. "I don't know. Maybe it's because I know how much I care. Other people, they just do it for the cash."

"I don't think that's true, Reg. I don't think nobody does it for the cash around here. There are hundreds of precincts to work in. Nobody chooses to be here unless they're driven by a cause, or are tied to the place somehow. They grew up here, or they fell in love here, or they got unresolved issues to settle, or they just want to do some good in a place that badly needs it. There are other dedicated cops to step up, Reggie. You've served your community – or whatever the hell you were trying to do. Now it's time to walk away."

"I don't think I ever could."

"Well, you know what? I think you should apply for a transfer to my precinct. Walk a few miles on my beat. See how it could be. I'll put in a good word for ya. Show you around. Point you in the right direction for a good partner. Benjy's got a cracking sense of humour. You could drive around – eat a donut, for Christ's sake – be a normal, everyday cop. You know, the sort that Rosie don't have to worry about, because you ain't gonna end up on the news for shooting or being shot. Be ordinary."

"I don't want to be ordinary."

And there I was. The truth. I was just like those kids, but on the other end of the spectrum. You see, deep down inside me, I had that same fear that I was going to disappear and be forgotten. To be born in a place that put you on the bottom of the heap from day one gave you this burning desire to not stay there. You had to move upwards, or stay where you were, but burn so brightly that nobody could miss you. You didn't want to live and die on the bottom of the pile. Yeah, that feeling was still in me. And it was probably the real reason I didn't want a nice, ordinary, safe beat – because there was no glory in watching traffic. No, it was out *there*, in the hood, where the threat was real, and doing the job right mattered. Where you might end up saving a life or taking a life on any given day. I enjoyed it. And that was why I could never give it all up for a quiet nine-to-five somewhere safer.

Winston sighed again. Shrugged again. "I don't know what you want me to say, Reg. You can't have it both ways. You either stay in the hood and suck it up when you feel like you're getting nowhere, or you take your work someplace else, where the streets are kinder. That's your call, but you don't get it both ways. That's life out here."

I thought about what he said, and took it home with me to Rosie. I guess I wasn't all that surprised when she took much the same view on the matter as Winston.

"I won't lie, baby. I understand what you're trying to do out there, and I have faith in you that you can do it – but, honestly, I'd sleep better at night knowing you weren't in a place where every kid's got a gun. In a place where having a badge meant something. And I don't think it's a sign of weakness to walk away."

"I dunno, Rosie. The only reason I became a cop was to go back to my old hood and make it better."

"And I think you've probably done that, Reg. But maybe what you thought was a life calling, was just something you were meant to do for a little while. I mean, does it mean any less to be out there protecting people in a different area?"

"In a different area, that'd be all I was doing – protecting them. But I wanted to do more than that. I wanted to inspire."

"Being a cop is a noble profession, baby. And you can inspire people to do that wherever you go."

I sighed heavily. "Maybe you're right. Maybe you're both right. Perhaps I'm getting to the end of what I'm gonna achieve in the hood. I've seen one whole generation of kids grow, and not one of them has changed a step on the path they were on because of me – or not in any way that I can see. If I'm really not making any difference, maybe I should just give up and put my own life and my own family first."

Rosie laid her hand gently on my shoulder. "I didn't say you weren't making a difference, baby. Just that you can make a difference somewhere else, too. You know that I'll stick by you, whatever you decide."

"I'll think about it, Rosie," I promised. "Maybe it's time we all moved on."

CHAPTER NINETEEN

S uicide. An obvious one. Freddy Jones had jumped to his death from the roof of his fourteenth story apartment building, and died on impact. We're always called out to such dramatic deaths as that, just in case there's been foul play, but it was clear what had been going through Freddy's head when he'd jumped. After twenty-five years of loyal service at the Sanitation Department, the council had laid him off due to budget cuts. He'd lost the only way he had of keeping a roof over the head of himself and his disabled wife, and I guess the thought of letting her down got too much for him.

I was called to the scene on April 23rd and arrived around 4:30pm. Me and my partner, JJ, had been on patrol just around the block, so we were the first to arrive. First on scene meant that nobody had been there first to cover up, so I got to see the whole sorry mess that is left behind when a body hits concrete after fourteen story fall.

There was no point doing CPR or even taking a pulse. Freddy was dead and in pieces on the ground. I didn't know his story then. He was just another black man, gone too young, but, as the story came together and I learned more and more about who he was and the life he had lead, the more and more unsettled I became, and the more and more I felt myself feeling like life just wasn't fair.

Freddy had lived an honest life. He was the model example of a kid done good. All his life he'd said 'no' to temptation. He'd turned down the drugs, and walked away from the violence. He'd kept his head low and not tried to fit into any gang. His momma had been proud of him.

Still, although a kid with a good heart and good intentions, Freddy wasn't a particularly gifted man, but that didn't stop him. He started at the bottom – the very bottom. Cleaning up the mess that others left behind on the streets. Sometimes cigarette butts, sometimes blood. Faithfully, day after day, he did his job to the best of his ability, as demeaning as it seemed. Eventually, he got promoted to manage a team of street cleaners, and, in time, he moved into the department offices, into logistics.

And there he'd stayed for twenty more years, working hard and getting the job done. Every piece of litter that was thrown down, Freddy made sure got picked up by someone. Every time the drains overflowed, Freddy made sure that someone got out there to stop the floods. He kept the streets clean in the most mundane of ways. The most ordinary of ways.

But, it wasn't enough. Someone decided that there were too many people on the logistics team, and Freddy was easy pickings without any qualifications to his name – not with young big shots with degrees commuting from the city. And so they laid him off. They didn't care about his disabled wife, or the home he'd earned that was sliding out of his grasp. They didn't care that Freddy couldn't afford the daily commute into the city to find a job in a similar line of work, or that he had no savings. They just didn't care.

And so he jumped. And I couldn't say I blamed him, because I felt his frustration and his pain. Freddy had been one the few who had done the *right* thing. He was one of the few who lived life the way we all preached it should be lived – ordinary, hard-working, honest, law-abiding. He'd settled down in a tiny apartment and started a family. He'd raised each of those kids well. So well that one of them had won a scholarship to a college. He'd fed his family every day of his life. He'd shown how clean living was possible, even in the ghetto.

And then, some cruel commander from above had ripped it all away from him and made it mean nothing. Freddy was dead and nobody would remember him except his grieving widow and children.

It made me lose all faith in this world and what I was preaching. I mean, who was I to tell kids out here that they should buckle down and make an honest living and pay their dues, when there was no saying that they'd ever seen any reward for such dedication. There were too many Freddys out there. Too many dead kids. Too many drug addicts and alcoholics. Too many drop-outs and convicts. The whole place was falling apart.

All my life, I'd tried to find hope out here in the hood. And where I couldn't see it, I'd decided to create my own. I'd worked and I'd toiled to see some kind of change here; some kind of light at the end of the tunnel, but, at the end of the day, we were all one bad day away from being another Freddy; another Leo. Freddy had done all the things that the system had told him to – and the system had cut his throat.

It seemed to be the fate of too many black men and women. So often, we'd be told to look backwards to see our history of slavery, but it was happening right now. Not in the same way as before, but, in a manner. Here we were, still slaving for the man, who would work us to the bone, and then be done with us. We were still giving every second of our time and every ounce of our energy into working to fulfil an endless workload, without ever seeing a change in our own status to feel like our work was progress. Before, we'd jumped from the slave ships to save us from our fates, and now we jumped from the roofs of apartment blocks.

I hadn't been myself for months – ever since Randall, ever since Freddy. I was still clinging onto some of my old conviction that change was possible, but I was losing that faith day by day. The final straw came for me one night when my cousin, Martel, came to stay with us on a visit from Jamaica. His little sister had followed her man over to America years ago, and had ended up where we all end up – in the hood. She was living in a tiny studio apartment with her man and their new baby, so Martel was staying with us.

One night during his stay, he went out to visit her.

"Are you coming?" he'd asked me. "Y'know Bella would love to see y'all."

"Thanks, Martel, but I'm exhausted. Give my love to your sister."

I'd let him walk out the door just like that, because I was too tired and too drained from another day banging my head against a wall to go and spend time with a cousin I hadn't seen in sometime. That was the last time I saw Martel. Actually, no. The last time I saw Martel was when I arrived at his sister's house after she called me, screaming hysterically down the phone, and I found him clinging to his neck in the street, a bullet through his neck.

From what I understand, it went down like this. Martel had been visiting his sister in her apartment block. On the other side of the street, a huge house party had been raging. Martel had stayed in with Bella and the baby, and had nothing to do with the party going on in the block. After his visit with his sister was done, he'd stepped into the street to walk home. He'd crossed over to the side of the street where the party was in full swing, and then, out of nowhere, he'd been shot right in the neck in a drive-by.

By the time I'd arrived after Bella had called me, I knew it was already too late, but I still tried to save him. I clamped my hands down over his throat on top of his. Blood was gushing out in angry, crimson spurts, and I'll never forget the way Martel's eyes were so wide that they were more white than dark irises and pupils; open wide as his mouth gasped for air. I was pressing down so hard to stop the bleeding that I didn't know whether I was saving him or choking him.

When the EMTs finally arrived, he was already gone. Bled out on the driveway. In the days that followed, it all came out that the shooters had had a feud with a different man, who happened to look a lot like Martel. A case of mistaken identity had been all it had taken to end an innocent life.

I'd had to be the one to break the news to Martel's Mom, my aunt. She'd cried and howled down the phone like I don't know what, and Rosie had had to grip my hand so tightly and keep her eyes fixed on mine to get me through that phone call, because all I wanted to do was run away.

My Aunt had cried, "Why did you let him go there, Reggie? He shoulda been safe with you."

Her words cut me like a knife. It seemed that I was letting a lot of people down lately. I was wearing a badge, but incapable of using its power. Left, right and center, people were dying around me. Whether I was the cause of their deaths, or just a witness, sometimes it felt hard to say. All I knew is that I was sick of seeing people too much like me dying young and for no good reason.

So, I went through with what I'd spoken about with Winston and Rosie and gave up on the hood. I took on the assignment of Richmond Heights instead, where everything was much quieter, much safer. I felt no thrill in it. No real sense of purpose. No real anything. But it was easy work, where I could go, do my shift and go home.

Rosie was thrilled that I had moved somewhere safer, and made sure I knew it by making sure I came home to a beautiful home-cooked dinner every night and by cuddling up close to me when we went to sleep each night. I knew she was happy, but I felt restless and unfulfilled. Every time I gave someone a ticket for jaywalking or some other minor infraction, I felt like a sell-out, because I knew, that just a short bus ride away, kids were killing each other with guns, and killing themselves with drugs. And yet, here I was, turning a blind eye and doing the easy beat.

Winston was pleased to have me working in his area and had greeted me that first day with a broad grin and a pat on the back. "Glad to have you at Richmond, Reggie. You won't regret it."

I already regretted it. My whole life, I had lived with one loyalty – to the community where I grew up. Good or bad, I'd taken whatever it had thrown at me and used the experience to grow stronger. Through that gritty community, I'd seen both sides of the coin - the grimy, impoverished and violent backstreets of the hood, and the pride and self-respect of wearing a badge. Now I'd turned my back on the home that had made me, and just because I'd grown tired of her betrayal.

I knew, logically, that I was doing the right thing. I was sure I'd go mad before long if I got called to one more crime scene where I had to stare at a dead body – whether that was a dead kid or another Freddy given up -, but in my heart, I knew that only those made in the hood could ever survive there.

So I don't know what I really felt during those days at Richmond Heights. Was I really happy there? No, not really – but I'd lost faith in my community and couldn't figure out what my place in it was anymore. So, while I tried to figure it out, being in Richmond Heights was as good a place to be as any. It was safer, at least, and gave me time to clear my head.

That's what I needed, after all. To clear my head. To breathe. Yet, it was hard for my head to feel clear when I couldn't shake thoughts of Leo, and Randall, and Freddy. The ghosts of so many on-the-job horror stories was weighing heavily on my back, and I didn't know how to get back the spark that had used to make me believe that I could be the one to change things.

So, for the time being, I made do. I lived that ordinary, glory-free life that I told others they should wish for, while all the while feeling like I'd lost the biggest part of me somewhere between my community, the line of duty, and everything that happened in between.

At least I had Rosie, and my kids, and that was a lot. They were my constant. There when I came home every day, no matter whether I was coming in from the dirty backstreets of the hood, or the pristine tree-lined avenues of Richmond Heights. There was that small miracle that made life worth living.

CHAPTER TWENTY

'd been at my lowest once before in life. Yes, there had been another time when I'd felt like I'd lost my forward momentum and didn't know where my future lay. That had been back when I'd been a kid and did something stupid to earn a quick buck. It had been when I'd got myself thrown in a detention center for armed robbery.

I'd recalled that feeling so many times in the years since; the way I'd felt the first time those bars had slammed shut behind me. Despair. Humility. Disappointment in myself. The feeling like it was game over. It had been the worst feeling I'd ever felt in my life, knowing that I'd thrown it all away and it was all my own damn fault.

You'd think you'd want to forget feeling something like that, but I'd always held onto it, because it reminded me why I stayed on the straight and narrow. I never wanted to feel that way again. It was remembering what it felt like to be at my very lowest point that kept me reaching for something higher. It was never wanting to feel that way again, and it was Charlie.

Charlie had been a volunteer at the detention center. A retired cop. He was one of those do-gooders that stayed in the hood instead of running from it. Even after his retirement, he still chased that urge to make a change.

Before getting locked up, I'd met many like him – the volunteers who came into the school to try and beg us to make a change, and the community workers who built activity centers and new basketball courts to try and keep us off the street. And none of them had ever got through to me until Charlie.

He'd been in his fifties back when I'd been a young offender doing my time. Old, by my young view, but young in his ways. He was black, like me, and became something of a role model and an inspiration while I was inside.

Charlie ran a sports team inside the detention center. It was something between athletics and rehabilitation, where we'd all play ball, but also use the sport as a way to take out our frustrations and learn to deal with our issues. And Charlie was like our big brother or uncle or something. Like some older relative that you looked up to.

At first, I didn't buy into his motivational talks and big speeches, but the longer I listened to them, the more I wanted them to be true. See, the thing is, when you're out there living life, you don't want to hear from someone that it can be better, because you don't think that 'better' is ever coming your way, and it sorta feels like these strangers are force-feeding you someone else's dream. But when you're on the inside, and you're trapped, you want to be fed that dream, because there's nothing else to keep you going except the hope that maybe you haven't screwed up so bad that you've thrown your life away. The hope that you can still somehow make your life matter.

So, I listened to Charlie and all his wise words over the weeks and months that I was inside.

He used to tell me, "Reggie, you always have a choice in this life. Left or right. Forwards or backwards. Up or down. Heck, even staying still is a choice. So many kids make the mistake of thinking that the circumstances they're in means that they ain't got no choices. Like, 'I'm poor, so I can't get an education'. That's a lie you tell yourself, Reggie. I mean, here you are, in the detention center, and you feel hard done by, because you're behind bars. You think it's everyone else's fault because they didn't do more. Well, you know what, kid? Tough. You made choices that got you in here, and now you've got to make your next lot of choices. So, what you gonna do Reg? Are you gonna waste the time you got in here feeling sorry for yourself and building up this hatred towards 'the man', or are you gonna use what you got right at your fingertips to pull yourself out of the hole you got yourself into? They got programs here. You could some learning in here. Learn a trade. Read. It's all there for you to take – if you choose."

That was what Charlie was all about- choices. Left or right. Up or down. Forwards or backwards. Stay still. Climb the ladder, or stay stuck at the bottom of the heap.

Over time his words began to sink in, and I began to believe them. Yes, I did have a choice. I could choose to carry on with the same old bad attitude and reckless behaviour, or, I could turn my back on everything that had come before and only look forwards.

It was Charlie that made me want to be a cop. For the first time, I saw someone in a position of power doing something good with it, rather than using it as a way to look down on everyone, and I realised that I could do some good too.

"I know lots of cops who do it for the money, or the respect, or the power, but the real good ones – the true blues – are the ones that do it because they got a calling deep inside. Some of 'em want to protect the innocent. Some of 'em want to bring the violent and the cruel to justice. Some of 'em just want to counteract all the chaos out there somehow. No matter what path in life you choose, Reggie, you ought to do it 'cause you've got something inside telling you it's right and that you're gonna make a difference. Now, all that gang life out there can make you think you've found that calling, but being called is not the same as having a calling. In life, you're gonna get a lot of voices all around you calling, calling, calling. 'Hey, Reggie – wanna try this?', 'Hey Reggie, do this!', 'Hey Reggie, bet you don't have the balls to jack that car!' The only voice you should listen to is the one that comes from deep inside, that tells you what you got to do to feel complete. Find a real calling, Reggie. Something that makes you feel like you're doing good."

And that's what I did. I found a calling that was a little bit of Charlie's idealism mixed up with a bit of my loyalty to my hometown that for a while gave me real purpose. It made me real happy. I was a true blue, serving my community and living out my calling.

So it felt like shit when I stopped doing that, but even walking the beat in the hood didn't feel right anymore. I wasn't living my purpose whichever streets I walked on, because I wasn't making a difference no matter what I did.

Maybe talking to an old friend could help me rediscover that calling. Maybe I could feel that spark of passion burning again if I could talk one true blue to another.

I didn't meet Charlie in a bar or café. That wasn't Charlie. No, Charlie welcomed you right into his home. That's where I went when I needed to rediscover my passion – Charlie's. I'd been there many times over the years. Charlie wasn't a person who rooted himself to places – he rooted himself to people. That meant it didn't matter where I was in the world, or what I was doing in my life – Charlie was always there.

It was Charlie who got me into the Police Academy even though I had a record. It was Charlie who kept pushing me when I was working hard for the first time in my life and feeling the pressure; feeling like I wanted to quit. It was Charlie who had the biggest grin on his face when I finally became a cop. And it was Charlie who had been there ever since when I was feeling lost or overwhelmed.

Poor Charlie never got enough return on the positivity and encouragement he gave out. I'd be lying if I said that I gave him as much as he gave me. Life just got in the way, you know? It was the same reason I'd not taken the time to watch out for Randall after Leo died. Life just for in the way.

Yet, Charlie was always there. It didn't matter if I went weeks without speaking to him, or months, or years… whatever time of day or night I called him, he answered the phone. I never needed an invite to show up on his porch – his door was always open. Charlie was always there for me. He was there for me now.

I rolled up to that familiar, worn-out but homely old house on the edge of the hood – far enough out that you could relax during the day, but close enough that you still kept your doors locked at night. Charlie was sitting in his front yard reading a newspaper when I arrived.

I smiled. Charlie never changed, although he got older. By that, I mean that maybe his hair grew grey and his wrinkles deepened, but his demeanour never aged – always smiling, always positive; no matter what life threw at him.

He was a slim man with dark skin and a thin smile. His hair was tightly curled and cut close to his scalp. His faced was marked with age-spots now. One or two more seemed to appear every time I visited him – but he was well into his sixties now. He was wearing a pair of dress pants and a button-up shirt with an open collar and sleeves rolled up, which looked funny against the pair of comfy slippers on his feet. He was sitting in a stripy deck chair, but rose to his feet with a kindly smile and open arms when he saw me.

"Reggie!" he greeted fondly. "It's been too long, son. Come, sit down with me."

I gave Charlie a one-armed hug and he slapped me on the back and then I sat down next to him on another one of those old stripy deck chairs. Charlie cracked open a cold one for me and we sat side by side to talk.

"So, Reggie, what's going on this time, hey? You only come to visit old Charlie when something's on your mind."

"That's not true."

Charlie laughed and held up a hand to quiet my objections. "Now, now, Reg – I don't mind. That's what I'm here for. C'mon, tell me what's going on."

I sighed and wondered where to begin.

"Is Rosie alright?"

"Oh yeah, she's fine."

"And the kids?"

"Doing well?"

"So, it's the job then."

I smiled. "Am I that easy to read?"

"There's only two things that have ever mattered to you, Reggie – your loved ones and your pride. Your family counts for the first, and your career was always what counted for the second."

"Well, you're right. I'm having trouble keeping my eyes on the goal, Charlie. I'm starting to wonder what's it all about... why am I in this game?"

"Oh, well that's easy enough to answer," Charlie said wisely. "You're loyal to your community, and you want to leave it better than you found it."

"Yeah, I did. Except I ain't leaving it no better. Don't you ever get the feeling like nothing ever changes?"

"What? No, Reg, I don't. I've seen too many happy endings to believe that anything's set in stone."

"You're the only one."

"You've got to put yourself in the right place at the right time to witness miracles. That's what I made my life about. I went to where I was most needed. To where people were down and out and ready to listen. 'Cause that's the trick, Reg. Nobody listens until all the other voices have gone quiet. Then you can be heard."

"Do you remember my friend, Leo?"

"I never met the young man, but I remember you telling me what happened. You were pretty cut up about it."

"He had a son."

"I remember."

"He's sixteen now."

"Is he?"

"Yeah. Got himself into some trouble lately. Got himself shot."

"I'm sorry to hear that."

"I tried to reach him before it happened. Then, when he got shot, I thought that was my chance to really get through to him. Just like you said – waiting for him to be ready to listen. But, he wasn't ready. Won't listen to a word I say. I reckon he's gonna end up dead out there, or locked up. He'll end up the same way as Leo."

"And it's eating at ya," Charlie guessed.

"Not just that. The whole thing – this whole job, that whole community. You try and try and try to make a change, but nobody wants to hear it."

"I get it, Reg. It's a tough crowd, but that's why we go there. What use is there in preaching to a choir? You can't reform someone who's already heading in the right direction. And that's why you chose that community; that's why you stuck with it – because there's a sense of satisfaction in cracking a tough nut that you just don't get from babysitting good kids. You like the feeling of doing something that nobody else can do."

"Maybe I would, Charlie, if I could do it either."

"Oh, I believe you can. I know you've got what it takes to get through to that boy."

"He don't want to know. Blames me for Leo's death."

"And what's his death got to do with you?"

"That stupid stunt we pulled was my idea."

"In my experience, kids who are pulling petty crimes always get pulled into the big game in the end. If it wasn't you, it would have been someone else."

"That's what Winston says."

"He's right."

"Well, either way, it kills me that Randall won't listen. I don't want to see him go the same way Leo did. I can't let another one go like that."

Charlie's face creased in sympathy and he patted my knee reassuring, and then reclined back in his chair with a peaceful look on his face. "Some things are just out of our control, Reggie. Some things that we really, really want to be able to handle are just too big for us. Keep trying – because that's all you can do – but at the end of the day, you have to accept that he's a young man with his own mind, and his own choices to make. Short of locking him up yourself, there's not much you can do to stop him making bad decisions. If he won't listen, you just got to hope he comes around in time."

"How did you do it? How did you manage to get through to so many?"

"Well, I don't think I ever did all that much, Reggie. I always found that those kids already had dreams and desires that they'd pushed down deep 'cause they believed all those things were out of their reach. I just found them when they thought it was all over and got them to cough up those dreams once more. I just had to convince them that it could really happen – but it takes work."

"These kids just don't want to hear it. Not from me. They don't believe that things'll ever change for them."

"It's hard, Reggie. It really is, and I don't know what to tell ya. It's a fine balance between making them embrace what's already in them, and shoving something they don't want down their throat. Getting through to kids who don't want to hear it is an art – and it's something you learn over time after a lot of mistakes and after watching a lot of them ignore your good advice and throw their lives away. You're young still. You're still learning that art. You're going to watch it end badly for a lot of kids before you develop whatever grit or skill it is that allows you to say it just right – the way they need to hear it."

"I need to develop it now. I need to get through to Randall."

"Maybe I can speak to him for you. Two heads are better than one, hey?"

I felt a weight lift off my shoulders and I smiled. "That sounds good, Charlie. Let's do that."

CHAPTER TWENTY-ONE

Charlie never got to speak to Randall, because Charlie died the next day of a heart attack. The doctors said it was just his age and family genetics, but I think part of it was down to just how big his heart always was – right to the end.

Man, I felt guilt in the days that followed. I'd gone to see Charlie and only done what I'd always done and talked about myself. I had to wonder if there was ever a time in Charlie's life when somebody was just there for him, rather than needing him to be there for them.

Charlie had been a widower for a long time. He'd been pretty much alone, in all the ways that counted. Sure, he spent a lot of time checking in on kids that he'd once helped out, or opening the doors of his home to people who needed him still; but, when Charlie had been out all day picking up the pieces of others' lives, there was never anybody for him to come home to. It made me real sad.

"I shoulda done more, Rosie," I lamented on the day I heard the news. "Charlie did so much for me, and what did I ever give him in return?"

"Charlie never wanted anything in return. That's what made him Charlie. He never did anything he did to get payback. He did it because it was what he was meant to do, and he loved doing it. Seeing you turn out good was all he ever wanted, baby. You made that man real proud."

"I can't help feeling like I'm just letting a whole lotta people down lately. I've always had this image in my head of myself as this sorta hero, out to save the hood from its own self-destruction, but that's not really what I am. I've just let myself build up an ego over the fact that I got out when others didn't, and taken on this saviour complex – but I'm no hero, Rosie. Charlie was a real hero. Do you remember that guy I told you about – Freddy? He was a hero. There's so many heroes out there, but I ain't one of them."

"Why have you got to be a hero at all? Why can't you just be Reggie? Just a normal guy with good intentions doing his part for the world? You don't have to save them all and you can't save them all. So maybe you took more than you gave when it came to Charlie, but nobody can say that you take more than you give when it comes to life. You're always out there giving, and clearing up other people's messes and trying to get through to kids who have nobody else to give them good advice. Charlie understood that. Charlie was the same."

Maybe Rosie was right, but it didn't help much. I felt terrible knowing that the last time I saw Charlie it was to whine and get things off my chest. I mean, we barely even spoke about Charlie. If we had, maybe I'd have known that he'd had some problems with his health lately; and maybe I'd have worked out that he didn't have all that much time left. But, I didn't – I wanted to talk only about me, and my dreams, and my failings. A lot of conversations seemed to be about me lately.

Rosie wasn't able to tell me what I needed to hear, although she tried to say the right things. So I decided to call on Winston, who might be able to speak to me one cop to another, to put things into perspective.

We met in the same bar as always. Was it just me, or was it ever dimmer and dingier than before? The low lighting and stained table tops seemed depressing somehow. You had to go down a flight of steps to enter the bar, and it felt like I would disappear underground forever.

Winston greeted me with a handshake and a slap on the back and we sat down to drink. He ordered a scotch; me, a whiskey. And we began to talk.

"Sorry to hear about Charlie, Reg. I know you two were close."

"Not as close as I thought. I didn't even know he was sick."

"If he'd have wanted you to know, he'd have found a way to tell ya."

"I should have asked."

"Charlie wouldn't have wanted a fuss."

"Still."

We both drank in silence for a while. I didn't really know what it was I needed to hear from Winston, but I knew I needed something. There had to be something that someone could say to break me out of this funk that I'd sunk into and get me back to my old self again; ready to face the world.

"I think I need to go back to the hood, Winston," I said at last. "This new beat is no good for me."

Winston frowned and gave me a stern look. "What do you mean, Reg? You're doing fine. The serge is impressed with you. You're one of us now."

"Impressed with me?" I scoffed. "For what? Writing out parking tickets with neat handwriting? Jesus, Winston, I'm going crazy in that area where nothing ever happens."

"I thought you were going crazy in the hood."

"Man, I think it's just me feeling crazy in general. Life's moving on and nothing's changing, y'know? It makes you question everything, like whether you're really doing anything at all. When I was on the beat in the hood I wasn't sure I was making a difference, but working on your beat, I know for sure I'm not. Nobody's life is gonna change for the better because I stop a kid tagging a brick wall with some spray paint. I was doing more before. At least another cop on the street might make a gang scatter now and then, and you and me both know that sometimes a shooting is all down to wrong place, wrong time. Making a gang scatter might save a life – you'd just never know it."

"So you've come full circle then? Back to your old self, huh?"

"Not my old self, no. Not even the shadow of my old self. All that's happened is that I've realised there's nothing new in a new place. The feeling's the same – like I'm doing nothing. But, you know me, Winston – my loyalty was always to the hood. It's in my blood.

As long as I'm away, I can hear it calling me. I've tried it your way. I've tried playing it safe; taking it easy. Now I know I gotta go back."

"What's Rosie got to say about that, huh? I thought she liked the fact that you were working a safer beat."

"Yeah, she does. But she also knows who I am. She knows what my makes me go. I think she knew that I'd always go back there in the end. When Charlie died, it started the cogs turning and we spoke about everything. We both know I've gotta go back."

"What is it about Charlie's death that convinced you to go back, when Freddy's death and your cousin's death all made you want to leave?"

That was a tough one to answer. I fell silent to think about it for a while. Eventually, I leaned back and looked at Winston contemplatively.

"You know, I think it's just that Charlie was the first one to make me believe in myself, and as I got older, I started to see him in me, and know that I had the same calling that he did. I feel like Charlie gave me a legacy to follow and I gotta be true to that. Charlie's not in the world no more, so I gotta step up. He always told me that getting through to kids is just a matter of experience and perseverance, and it takes one or the other – or both – to make a difference. In time, I'll learn the lessons I'll need. In the meantime, it's all about perseverance."

"You know, I'd be lying if I said I'd never thought about going back there myself," Winston confessed to me. "I know you think I sold out long ago, but you know, after all we'd done to claw our way out of that place, I thought we'd earned a better life. I thought I deserved a nice home, in a nice area, and a safe job. I thought my wife and kids deserved better than I had. But I still remember why we got into this game. It was always about making that place better. You know, ever since you came to me with that whole thing about Leo's kid, it's got all those old feelings coming back again. Y'know, the desire I used to have to change the world. I'm feeling like I could use a change right now. My kids aren't babies no more. I feel like it ain't wrong to take those risks, like it was back when they were born.

Reggie, I think I might just follow you back there while I'm in my prime. Save the safe beat for when I'm old and grey. Apply for your transfer Reggie – and tell your station that I'm on my way, too."

All things told, it wasn't a bad day for a funeral. The weather was fine; cool, but clear, and dry. The churchyard where Charlie was being buried wasn't all that much to look at, but I knew that it was the church that he went to every Sunday. And my lord, what a turn out there was that day. It seemed that every person in a fifteen-mile radius had showed up to see Charlie off, and it made my heart so glad.

I'd worried and felt guilt over the fact that Charlie had done so much and got so little in return, and yet, here it seemed like the whole world had turned up to say goodbye. It just went to show how small ripples turned into waves somewhere down the line, and that Charlie had been a tsunami of goodness that had washed a whole generation onto better things.

There were people of all ages there. Many my own age; some older, some younger. I'd bet that many of them had passed through the prison system, like me, or been down and out in some other way before Charlie found them. Many of them seemed to be doing alright now. They were there with their families. Lots of them were wearing nice suits – the kind you couldn't afford if things weren't going your way. The crowd was polite, and warm and supporting each other; and in each kind word and gesture of comfort I saw Charlie. He'd taught so many how to open up their hearts and minds to have faith in themselves and others, and the effect of that teaching was so evident here, now that everybody was living by the principles that Charlie had preached. On such a sad day, the presence of so many mourners who still carried Charlie in their hearts made it special, somehow. It was clear just how many lives Charlie had touched, and it inspired me to do the same. Experience and perseverance. I hear you Charlie… One day, I'll make just as much of a difference. By your guidance, and my grit; we'll get there, Charlie.

CHAPTER TWENTY-TWO

First day back on the beat in my old community and I hear somebody's name keep popping up – Randall. I'd hoped that after the trouble that boy had got himself into, that he'd have learned his lesson, and at least kept his head down, if he couldn't find a way to get out of the place and his lifestyle altogether. But, no luck. From what I was hearing, Randall was back out on the streets, rolling with the same crowds he'd been rolling with just before he got himself shot last time.

I say 'last time' because I knew all too well that when you decided to live in the danger zone, you put yourself in harm's way every day. Sooner or later, Randall's luck would run out. Just like it had done for Leo.

I knew that Randall was desperate to live with a target on his back, but I could only hope that maybe – with God's help – I could find a way to save him before the next person fired. He wouldn't listen to me. He wouldn't listen to his principal or teachers. He wouldn't listen to his Grandma. But maybe he'd listen to his mother.

It didn't take much to track her down – just a chat with Flo – but, convincing her to come back here was more difficult. That phone call had been a difficult one to make.

I tried to conjure up the face of the girl that I'd only met once or twice when we'd been young. She'd been a fairly pretty thing, back then, with her hair often in numerous braids that fell down to the base of her spine. I remembered that she'd been a bold and contentious young woman, who always stood her ground; fiery. I remember the first time I met her and how I thought a woman with that much energy and ferocity would never get by with someone like Leo, who was all mouth and ego. I thought they'd clash, and argue – which they did, often. But, somehow, it worked for them. They argued, but then they kissed and made up, and were no worse for it. The pair of them were a lot of noise, but underneath all that was also a lot of love.

I'd never thought that a stubborn and brazen woman like Hannah would ever be right for an equally stubborn and egotistical guy like Leo, but it turned out that it worked. Hannah wouldn't take any of Leo's crap, and Leo respected Shannon for holding her own. Shannon was one of the only people who could ever calm Leo down and get him thinking straight. In time, she might have been a positive influence on him and got him on the straight and narrow.

Time. That's all the pair of them would have needed to make it all fall into place – time. Shannon's brother owned an autoshop, and he'd promised to give Leo a job there once he'd got out the joint. I don't know if a normal nine-to-five would have been right for Leo, but if anyone could have got him to give it a shot, it would have been Shannon. Leo thought the world of that girl.

Shannon must have thought the world of him too, because she never found another man after Leo died, which surprised me. I'm sure she could have had her pick of men if she'd have wanted, but she'd never wanted anyone but Leo.

I know she'd dreamed of having a happy life with him after he got out. In her mind it was all planned out – the three of them, living a normal life somewhere in the hood, where they kept their heads down, had the odd argument, but overall lived for those normal family moments that make it all worthwhile.

I dialled the number that Flo had given me, and finally, spoke: "Shannon?"

"Who's this?"

"It's Reggie. You might not remember me."

"I remember you alright. You're the one that had the bright idea to go guns blazing into a factory on the heist that got Leo put away. Yeah, I remember you."

Her words stung, but I suppose she had a right to say them. What she said was true after all. It *had* been my idea, and the only defence I had was that I'd been young and dumb and too keen to follow the example of so many who'd gone before me. I'd wanted to earn some street cred and buy my mum something new. I'd never wanted it to end the way it had.

"How you doing, Shannon?"

"How'd you think I'm doing, Reggie? I'm trying to make changes. I'm trying to do right by my kid."

"I know he's living with his Grandmother now."

"And how'd you know that?"

"I've had some run-ins with Randall lately. I'm a cop now, you know."

I could almost hear her eye's rolling down the phone line.

"Yeah, I heard it all worked out for you in the end. Alright for some, ain't it?"

"Look, this ain't about me. I called to try and get you on my side. Randall ain't doing so well."

"Yeah, I know. I'm his mother, in case you forget. Stupid kid got himself shot. He's doing alright now through, from what I hear. What is it you want from me, Reggie?"

"He's doing alright, sure, if you mean he ain't gonna drop down dead from that bullet wound any time soon, but he's not doing alright really, Shannon. He's started rolling with the same crowd again, and it won't be too long before he's looking down the barrel of a gun again. We got to act now if we want him to choose a different path."

"'We'?" Shannon scoffed. "Since when has anything ever been 'we', Reggie? Who do you think you are to talk about 'we'? I ain't seen you since before Leo died. You ain't nobody to me."

"I know that, and I'm sorry. I wasn't there for you or Randall when Leo died, but I'm trying to make up for it now. Back then I was a stupid kid who didn't know what to do in the face of such big problems. Y'know, how do you start a conversation like that? How do you put yourself back into the life of somebody who wants nothing to do with ya? How do you start to apologise for something like I made happen? I ran away from what happened and the face that it happened 'cause of me, and I tried to make amends through other kids heading Leo's way. But, I know it's time to start fixing things a bit closer to home. That means reaching out to Randall. I know I ain't been there to watch him grow up, or nothing like that, but he's Leo's kid, and that means something to me, 'cause Leo was like my brother."

"I know you're sorry, Reggie, but it don't change nothing," Shannon sighed. "It don't bring Leo back and it don't change the fact that Randall's just like him. It don't change the fact that I'm no good to him. He's so angry at me, Reg. He won't listen to me."

"It's worth trying. I know it is. Won't you come back and try and get through to him?"

"He won't talk to me. He thinks I didn't want him here. Truth is, I was just trying to get him out of harm's way while I was in self-destruct mode. No... he wouldn't want to see me. Besides, Reg, I don't want to go back there. Too many bad memories."

"Please, Shanon – I'm not asking for me. I'm asking for Randall. He needs you right now."

"And what is a kid with problems gonna think about advice coming from a woman with problems of her own? I've drunk too much in front of that kid. I've done drugs in front of that kid. I ain't the role model that's gonna make him think it's worth turning it all around."

"He don't need a role model. He needs his Mom. Just someone who cares about him to tell him that they want better for him. Better than the life they had. Better than his father had. It'll mean more coming from you. He don't believe for a second that I care, even though I do."

Shannon thought for a long while, and then finally sighed. "Fine. I'll get a bus down there. But don't expect no miracles, Reggie. My boy just don't work like that. He don't want to be saved."

It was an intervention – if you could call it that. Me, Flo and Shannon waited at Flo's house for Randall to come home. Flo said it was hard to tell when he'd next be by. Sometimes he went two, three days without stopping in – and God knows where he went on those nights. We had no choice but to wait.

There was tension amongst the three of us. I could tell that Flo was mad with Shannon and Shannon was mad at Flo, and there I was caught in the middle, just trying to do some good for a change.

"I thought sending Randall here would do him some good," Shannon muttered to herself, but definitely loud enough that Flo could hear her.

The old woman puckered her lips in response and scowled. "And why would you think this place would do him any good? It didn't do you so good now, did it?"

"Well, I thought he'd be better off with his grandma."

"I'll love the boy, but I'm no miracle worker. Some would say the damage was already done."

"And what's that supposed to mean?"

"That boy needed his mother."

"He needed his father."

Then I felt like both pairs of eyes were on me and I didn't know what to say. It was exhausting to feel like I needed to apologize a thousand times for something I did so long ago that hurt so many, but I knew that my apologies would change nothing. It wouldn't bring Leo back to his loved ones, and it wouldn't shift any of this guilt that I'd carried for so long.

"He needs anyone who cares enough to set him straight," I said at last. "Mother, father, grandmother – it doesn't matter. We're all voices telling him the same story. Turn it around, or throw it all away."

"Reggie's been watching out for that boy while you've been doing whatever the heck you've been doing away from here," Flo told Shannon pointedly. "He's been the one out there chasing him down to stop him getting into trouble, and visiting him in hospital and checking in with his principal to see how he's doing. At times, he's been the only one watching out for him."

"Again, Mom, what are you trying to say? You know why I made the choices I made. Randall was always better off without me. I was just trying to get him away from something bad for him."

"Only to throw him into another situation that's bad? You remember what it was like here, Shannon. Anywhere's better than here."

"That's not true. Some folk turn out just fine."

"Yeah, they do. The ones who have parents who show them the way."

"You're always trying to pin the blame on me. Ain't I the one who took him away from here in the first place? I tried to do right by him, but I wasn't strong enough alone. I thought I was doing right by admitting that. Sending him away was hard for me. You know, it was Randall who always picked me up when I passed out with a bottle in my hand. It was Randall who let me cry my heart out on my shoulder. It was Randall who made sure there was food in the cupboards. If I'd've been selfish, like I wanted to be, I'd have never let him go. My boy took care of me. He kept me company. It ain't easy being on my own, but I know that he deserves better than to be his momma's babysitter."

Flo shook her head in disgust. "They all deserve better than what we give 'em."

"You've been mad ever since the day I got pregnant with him."

"Damn right I have, Shannon," Flo snapped. "There you are talking about doing right by your kids and setting them straight – and what d'you think I tried to do for you? I tried to give you an education, and a path in life, but you went sleeping around with bad news, and the cycle just continues. It just takes one person in the chain to have the brains to do it different, and then the chain is broken. We could have better lives – or, at least, our kids could."

"Leo wasn't 'bad news', Mom. He was just young and dumb. Like we all were. Like you were once."

"I just didn't want that for you."

"Yeah, Mom. I know. But it happened. A lot of stuff happened. I'm trying to move past it and do better. Can't you?"

I listened to them talk and felt sad at what I was hearing, because their story wasn't theirs alone. It was the story of so many out here. So many young people and their parents started out determined that they were gonna make the change that would lead the future generations onto better things, and so many made one bad choice or one mistake somewhere down the line that sent all their good intentions into a tailspin.

I felt sorry for Shannon, because I think her only mistake had been falling in love with a reckless man. She'd been swept up in Leo. Shannon was as much of a thrill-seeker as he'd ever been, but whereas Leo had found his thrills in petty crime and street battles, she found hers in the passion of an angry young man.

Sure, there were different choices she could have made with her head, but I think there had only ever been once choice for her in her heart – Leo. Their love was an intense flame that burned brightly, and flickered in Shannon still, even though the one who'd set that flame burning was long gone. Now she was trying her damnedest to give her son some of the same devotion she'd once shown Leo, and to stand by him as he made reckless decisions.

As if reading my mind, Shannon began to speak about him. "I always thought that Leo would come back to me, y'know. I didn't think that I was just waiting for him to get killed in there, or locked away again. I always thought I was just holding on until he came back for good. He made so many promises to me, y'know. He promised me he'd stay on his best behaviour and try for early release. He promised me that once he was out, he'd take the job Billy was gonna give him and hold it down. He promised me he'd provide for me and Randall. He promised me that when he'd saved enough money, he'd buy me the biggest damn diamond ring the hood had ever seen and make me his wife. I believed him, and I was waiting for him to keep all those promises. Stupid man – if he'd have kept them, he'd still be here."

A sad, nostalgic smile hovered at my lips. "That was just Leo, though. He had no self-control."

"You're right about that. No damn control at all. And Randall's just the same."

"If I remember rightly, though, you were always able to get through to Leo."

Shannon sighed. "Once. But Randall's not the same. He's my son. I'm his mother. And I've let him down so many times before, that how can I blame him for doing his own thing?"

"Mom?"

I turned around to see Randall standing at the end of the drive, with his hood pulled up and that heavy jewellery rattling around his neck. He had a backpack slung over one shoulder and his baggy paints slung low around his waist. He was dressed like trouble, but his eyes were childlike when they spotted his Mom.

"What are you doing here?"

"Reggie called. He's worried about you."

"That ain't true."

"So it ain't true you got shot then?"

"You'd know if you ever called."

"I know, Randall. I check in on you, even if you don't know about it."

Randall frowned. "And why shouldn't I know about it?"

"I promised you I'd keep my distance until I'd sorted myself out."

"Well, you're breaking that promise. Look at you. You look like shit."

Shannon drew in a sharp, hurt breath and bit down on her lip. It was true. It was clear that she hadn't been taking proper care of herself. There were big dark circles under her eyes, but the rest of her skin was pale. Her once braided hair was now loose and straggly; thin and cut to shoulder length. Her face was gaunt, so that she looked haggard with sunken cheeks. A figure that had once been attractively slim was now skeletal and ill-looking. There were track marks on her arm.

"I'm three months sober."

"I've been here eight months."

"I had a relapse."

"No surprise there."

"Three months is a long time for me, baby."

"Not in my whole lifetime, it ain't."

"You're right. But I'm trying. I'm really trying."

Randall took a couple of steps closer as he began to talk with his Mum, but still kept his distance. He put his backpack down on the ground, folded his arms across his chest, and leant back against the rickety old picket fence behind him.

"So, what you really doing here then? Trying to talk me straight?"

"Someone's gotta try."

"This guy already did." Randall nodded towards me, and rolled his eyes. "But I don't need no good advice from nobody, Mom. What happened was just a misunderstanding. It's all over and done with and there's nothing going on now. I'm not doing nothing to cause a fuss. I'm just going about my business; nothing special."

"The guys you're hanging with are trouble, Randall," I chipped in. And I wasn't lying. Randall was hanging with a guy named Cody, and another they called Butch. Cody already had two priors under his belt – aggravated assault and wounding with intent – and Butch was a well-known name around the station. It seemed that no matter who was pulled in, they were always connected to Butch in some way or another. They were older guys with bigger attitudes, and they were trying to suck Randall in to their life of crime. "Do you know the kind of stuff they are into?"

Randall shrugged. "So what? Who hasn't done something they shouldn't 'round here? That's just part of living in the hood. You do what you have to."

"Do you *have* to hold a mother and her teenage daughter at gunpoint while you mug the husband and father? That's not a survival situation, Randall – that's a choice. That's a violent, criminal choice. The sort of choice you don't have to make."

He scowled. "You think that chirping about their priors is gonna make me think twice about rolling with them, Reg? Truth is, those guys have been there for me more in the last eight months than my own mother was my whole life – more than anybody ever was."

"And that's how they pull you in, Randall. People like them know just what people like you have been missing out on, and just what you want, and they make it seem like they can give it to you. Want a family? Check – they'll be your family. Need cash? Check – they'll hook you up. Need a thrill? Check – they'll make you feel alive. But really, what they're doing is pulling you onto a life that you don't want to walk down, and you won't even realize it until it's too late."

"So what would you have me do, Reg?" Randall challenged sarcastically. "Go to school and study like a good boy? Volunteer at some food bank? Visit the old folks' home on a Sunday? Go to church? You're kidding yourself. Nice guys end up on one side of a gun, and smart guys end up on the other."

"Nice motto, kid," I scoffed, "talking about being on the right side of a gun. What side of a gun were you on recently?"

Randall got real angry at that, and pointed a finger at me menacingly. "You got no idea what you're talking about, so just shut your mouth and stay out of it. In fact, stay out of my life. Stop following me. Stop asking 'bout me. Stop dragging up my past, and digging up family members and shoving your holier-than-thou shit down my throat. It's not gonna fly. You think I'm some helpless schoolkid, but I ain't. I've had burdens on my shoulders since I was a little kid, and that made me grow up fast. I'm making my own choices now. I'm gonna stick with the ones who stood by me. To hell with the rest of you."

With that, Randall picked up his backpack, sneered at us all one last time, and marched straight back down that path and out of sight. I didn't chase him. There was no point.

Shannon let out a long, shaky breath and put her head in her hands. "That went just as I expected."

"At least you tried."

"All we did was piss him off."

"He was already pissed off."

"That boy is gonna go out just like his father," Flo predicted, with a slow shake of her head. "Lord knows, he's my blood and I love him, but I'd be a fool to think that he's gonna last long on the road he's on. I gotta prepare myself for that."

Again, her words made me feel so full of sorrow. I couldn't help but feel that it was so wrong that a grandmother was so tired of reaching out, that instead she was preparing herself to say goodbye to her grandson. But what could any of us do? How can you bring back someone who's gone so far off the rails and is so determined to stay there?

"I'm sorry," I told them both. "I really hoped that something would come of this, but there's only so much we can do."

And there it was – those words I hated, and out of my own mouth. *There's only so much we can do.* I hated to say them, and I hated even more to know they were true. I felt drained, and out of options. I'd tried educating Randall with inspirational speeches at his school and one-on-one talks when I could get to him. I'd tried warning him. I'd tried sharing my own story with him. I'd tried getting through to him through his family. I'd tried watching over him like a hawk. In all honesty, I felt like I'd tried everything, and that maybe even perseverance wasn't going to solve this one. Randall was determined to choose his own path, and as long as all those people he resented and blamed for his troubles were telling him to go one way, he was going to go the other. So maybe it was time to stop pushing, and let Randall learn through the consequences of his own actions. We could only hope that he'd survive those consequences. There was nothing left to do but let him go his own way.

CHAPTER TWENTY-THREE

I tried to put Randall to the back of my mind in the weeks that followed, but it was tough. I knew that he was out there somewhere digging his own grave, and it broke my heart. I wanted to do more, but Randall was right – he had to make his own choices. That meant it was time to focus my efforts on all the many, many kids out there who might just make it if the right person would show them the way. After all, Randall's story was just one story amongst many.

I thought back over my life and all the influences – good and bad – that had shaped me. The bad influences had been many: poverty, my peers, the crime all around me, the desperate need for street cred, the skin I'm in, boredom, self-pity. The good influences had been far fewer: my parents, Charlie, and maybe some small little voice deep down inside of me that whispered that this wasn't what I wanted.

I wondered how much of a difference it would have made if there had been more good influences, or whether we were all destined to walk a crooked and dangerous path from the day we were born into the hood. Luckily, I'd been able to take a sharp turn away from that life, but for others, it was only a long drop down.

In the station and on the beat, I still heard Randall's name a lot, and the name of the boys he was rolling with. Cody and Butch were always getting into some scrap or another. One day, Cody got picked up for being in the wrong place at the wrong time. We had nothing solid to hold him on in the end, but it did give me a chance to have a word with him while he was on his way out.

Cody was a slim white boy with short blonde hair and thick eyebrows that always drooped sullenly over his hazel eyes. He wore a baggy white vest and track pants and the same excessive chains that Randall was so fond of. I caught him leaving the precinct out of the corner of my eye and I beckoned him over. Cody rolled his eyes and lingered for a moment. I wasn't sure that he wasn't going to ignore me and keep on walking straight out that door, but then he stopped, and reluctantly came over.

"What? Forgot to take prints or something?"

"Nah. I don't need nothing like that. I want to talk to you about something."

"I don't even know you."

"But I know you, and the crew you hang around with. Butch, right? Bad news, he is. Done a lot worse than you have."

"So? What you trying to tell me? Want me to rat on him, is that it? Well, you're outta luck. I don't know nothing, and I'm not saying nothing."

"I'm not asking you to rat on nobody," I told him, and I gestured for him to come with me into an empty office, where we could talk in private. He did. "I wanted to talk to you about the new guy in your crew."

"Lil Smooth?"

"Yeah. That's the one."

"What about him?"

"You know he's a good kid, right?"

Cody scoffed and smirked. "Ah whatever."

"Sure, he's no angel, but compared to some out there, he's not too far gone, if you know what I mean. He's still got a chance. You know, he's got a Mom that really cares about him."

"That's not what I hear."

"Sure, she's made mistakes, but she loves him, and don't want to see anything bad happen to him."

"Why you telling me this?"

"I know from experience that people will make a lot of dangerous and stupid choices just 'cause their crowd tells them to. They'll get themselves into a lot of trouble just to fit in, or because the leader of their group gives them order."

"Yeah, some might."

"Well, what I'm saying is that I don't want that to happen to Smooth. At the moment he's got a clean record and a mom that's trying to better herself so that she can look out for him better. If he wanted, he could get out of here and make something of himself. But, that's never gonna happen if he starts making bad choices now, and starting trouble, and getting caught doing stupid things. You know what I'm saying?"

"And what's so special about Lil Smooth that you'd look out for him?" Suddenly, Cody's eyes widened. "I bet he's your rat, ain't he? Trying to keep one of your own safe, are ya?"

"Trust me, Cody, I got bigger troubles than Butch and his cronies." I shook my head. "No, Smooth's father was a friend of mine. You know how it is. Your crew's family is your family. I'm just trying to look out for a friend's kid. I don't want him to come to no more harm. Not after all that's already happened."

"That was all just a big misunderstanding. It's sorted now."

"So I hear. But talking from experience, one misunderstanding is never the end of it. There'll be other misunderstandings, and more, and more, until someone walks away."

Cody shrugged. "I ain't his keeper. If Smooth wants out, that's his choice. But I don't think that's gonna happen any time soon."

"You're not a bad guy either, Cody. I know that. You've got little brothers, ain't you?"

"I don't see them no more. They got taken away."

"Well, imagine that they were out there gang banging. What would you tell them?"

"Hell, I don't know. I don't really think about them no more. I just think about me, and what I'm gonna do to survive."

"Yeah, I know that feeling, but sometimes you gotta think bigger than yourself, and bigger than today. Nothing ever gets better for nobody if we all just do the same shit over and over again. Look, all I'm saying is that I want you too look out for him if you can. And you know what? If you were smart, you'd turn back too, because you're not too far gone either. Look, you know where to find me Cody. If you want a hand to make a change, then I'm your guy. I'll hook you up. We're connected to all kinds of programs and support. You could learn stuff, get a real job – get out."

"I don't think so," Cody replied doubtfully. "'Cause I don't agree. I think I am too far gone. But I tell ya what, I'll keep an eye out on your boy for ya. Not because he's your boy, but because he's rolling with our crew now – like you said, that makes him family."

"I appreciate it."

Cody left and I didn't know if I felt better or worse for speaking to him. What was wrong with this kids? They were all just so disillusioned and so convinced that the lives they were leading were unchangeable and so definite. Even when you reached out and offered a different path, they resisted, and told you that there was no other way. Even when you opened a hundred other doors, they'd shake their heads and tell you that their path was predestined – they had to follow in the footsteps of everyone who'd come before, even knowing where that path had taken them.

After my talk with Cody, I went to find Winston. True to his word, he'd transferred to our precinct, and it was good to have him around again. Sure, we'd drifted over time, but whatever had made us such strong friends once before was still there underneath all the distance that time had put between us.

It turned out that Winston was a natural on this beat. He had that same kind of knack for making kids listen that Charlie had once had, and that I longed to have. Maybe it was time away from the place that made him do so well now that he was back. Winston had this kind of calm about him that I'd never felt, because I was always frantically trying to fix problems left, right and center, and save a hundred lives before it was too late. Winston came at things from a different angle; laid-back, cool, collected. Charlie had been like that - able to make you feel relaxed and like choices were just choices, and not life and death. Maybe I went at things too strong. Maybe I pushed too hard. Who knew?

Winston was sitting at his desk in the area we called 'the pen'. The pen was a place with a hundred different cubicles all crammed together; cell phones constantly ringing, cops all shoulder to shoulder, chasing leads and filing paperwork. Winston was sitting at his own desk, filling in some form or another. I went and sat on the edge of his desk and he leaned back in his chair and smiled at me.

"Busy day today, huh?"

"Sure is, Winston. Just been speaking to Cody."

"Butch's boy?"

"That's the one."

"And?"

"He said he'd keep an eye out on Randall for me."

Winston rolled his eyes, but his smile was sympathetic as he shook his head in exasperation. "I thought you said you were gonna drop it with Randall? He don't want nothing to do with us. He wants to learn the hard way."

"We both know that he's not gonna walk away forever from the kind of scraps he's getting himself into. He's into far more dangerous stuff than we ever got involved in. What did we ever really do? Until that stupid heist that got us busted, we were nothing but stupid teens pulling dumb stunts; vandalising, stealing drinks and chips from the store, getting into fist fights... Randall's in deeper waters. There's drugs, and guns and God knows what else going on around him. I can't just leave him on his own out there."

"He's not alone, Reg," Winston told me. "He knows we're here if he wants to find us. He knows where his grandma is, and his mom. He's choosing to turn his back on everyone trying to help him. He's choosing to play the role of abandoned teen. We went through that phase too, of feeling like the world had turned its back on us, when really we just weren't ready to take responsibility for ourselves. He's still young, and he's angry. I think, in time, he'll realize he's being dumb and start hearing us out."

"No, you're wrong. I don't think he'll come to it on his own. I don't think he'll reach eighteen and just suddenly snap out of it. He's too much like Leo. Too ready to start a fight. Too eager to earn his street cred. He'll get killed. I know he will."

"Well, asides from putting him away, there's not much you can do to prevent that, Reg. And even if we did bring him in on some petty charge and put him away for six months, you know that it's hit-and-miss trying to snap someone out of it in juvy. Sure, some kids come back down to earth with a bang and change their ways, but most of them just end up mixing with kids way worse than they ever were, making new contacts you don't want to make, and learning some new tricks to take right back out into the world with them. Putting him away might set him straight, but it might throw him in deeper. Besides, if getting shot wasn't the wake-up call he needed, then I don't think juvy will be either. You gotta face it, Reg: you've done all you can."

I hated knowing that. I hated it. I didn't want to give up on Randall – or any of them. Why did there always have to be a ceiling? Why did there always have to come a stage when you just ran out of options? I wanted to just scoop that kid up off the street and put him somewhere safe and far away until he matured enough to wise up. Except, I thought there was just too damn much of Leo in him to really believe that he'd ever wise up. Randall was programmed to find a thrill, just like Leo had been.

And so, I had no choice but to continue doing what I'd been doing so far, and just keep watching over him from a distance, and looking out for the perfect opportunity to try again. And while I didn't know whether getting Randall put in a cell would do him any good, I was pretty certain that getting Butch put away would at least give Randall a chance to walk away. Peer pressure was a real and deadly thing in these parts, and I wanted to take away the ring leader of Randall's group so that pressure was gone from him, and he could take off those rose-coloured glasses that made him think that being in a gang and having a crew was something so damned special.

So, I watched over Randall, and I reached out to Cody, and I plotted against Butch. And that was my three-way attack that I kept going for weeks, and for months. It was all I could do. But would it be enough?

CHAPTER TWENTY-FOUR

M e and Rosie sat out on the bench-swing on out back porch. It was a cold night. Christmas wasn't too far away now, and my mind should have been on festive, happy things; but, as usual, it was deep in thoughts of my civil duties and my friend's son.

"Baby, stop thinking about work," Rosie begged me. "Every night you come home with that look on your face. You gotta put it to rest, baby. You've got your own family to think about."

"I know, Rosie. You're right. I'm sorry."

Rosie sighed. In the past, she'd often sighed, but her sighs had been accompanied with a fond smile, or playful nudge, but now she was growing tired. "You say you're sorry, but I know you're going to be just the same tomorrow night. I don't know what to do with you these days, Reggie. When you're working in that area you're up to your neck in worry every night – so far away from me -, but when you were working that beat in a safer place, you just weren't yourself. It was like your spark had gone. This community or that community… it makes no difference. I just feel like I've lost you."

I turned to her and gripped her hands in a panic. Rosie was the most faithful, most intelligent and most beautiful woman I'd ever met. She was my world, and I adored her. To think that she felt I was letting go of her was a terrible, terrible thought. If I lost Rosie, my everything would be gone. There would be no lighthouse to call me home each night after a long and unrewarding shift. There would be no foundations to build my life on. There would be no warmth or companionship – just a lifetime of trying to fix other people's lives, while my own life fell to pieces.

"Please don't think that, Rosie," I begged her. "I love you now more than I ever have and I never want to lose you. I'm sorry I've been so far away for so long. I wish I knew how to change it."

Rosie sighed again and turned her gaze upwards, to the sky. "I still remember when I first met you. How handsome you were in your uniform. How alive you were. Do you remember? You told me that you'd never followed a dream in your whole life, and that now you'd made one come true, everything was going to be perfect." She smiled, a nostalgic smile, and I was drawn into the sweetness of her familiar lips. So beautiful. "I remember how much I admired your passion, and how much it drew me towards you. You were so alive back then. But something's changed, baby. It's not a passion anymore – it's an obsession. You used to do it because you loved it, and now you do it because you feel like it's your duty."

"You're right, baby. I know you're right, but I don't know how to fix it."

"You can start by just switching off for one night. Tonight, it is not your duty to fix someone else's life. Tonight, it is not your duty to save a kid from a bad choice. Tonight, it is not your duty to pick up broken pieces. Tonight, is for you, and for me, and for your family. And I pray to God that time you spend with us is because you want to, not because you feel it's your duty."

"I love you, and I love our kids. That's never been in doubt. You're my rock. You always have been."

Now she smiled. She put her hand on my cheek and held my gaze with hers. "Good. Then let's go inside and have dinner as a family. Then let's watch a movie – one with no cops in – and just pretend we're a nice, normal family."

"I'd like that."

And that's exactly what we did. We ate a nice dinner together that Rosie had cooked from scratch, and I made sure to really taste it. The flavours brought back memories of how special Rosie's dinners had been to me back when we'd first become a couple, and I felt so blessed to have someone care so much and take such good care of me. And we laughed, and I soaked it all up, because my bones were aching for some laughter. And we talked, and I relished in it, because it had been so long that a conversation was about nothing more than normal, ordinary, light-hearted stuff.

It was a wonderful evening, with a family that I had let take second place for too long. I felt myself relaxing for the first time in a long time, and remembering what it was all about a little. Sure, saving others had been a calling for me, but what was it all worth if I hadn't truly saved myself? Because that's where it had all started, after all. It had all started the day that I took the help that Charlie had offered me and chose a better life for myself. What was I doing letting myself get drawn back into the troubles and downfalls of the hood, when I'd worked so hard to get away?

I needed to learn to do my best for the people I was working so hard to help, but also remember that those troubles weren't mine any more. I didn't need to carry those burdens any more. How could I help anyone, if I got caught up in all their issues?

No, I was going to learn to give myself a break and try to strike a balance somehow between saving the world and living the life I'd worked so hard to have for myself and for my family.

CHAPTER TWENTY-FIVE

The call came in on a Friday morning on what had been an otherwise pretty quiet day. There had been a couple of everyday drug busts, and I'd shooed away a few kids from loitering in gang spots, and done the paperwork for a few drunk and disorderly cases, but nothing major.

The voice on the radio told me that this was a shooting. I felt a tired exasperation inside of me. I thought of Randall. I thought of Leo. I thought of my cousin. If I was meant to feel something more than disappointment and frustration, I didn't feel it right then, because I was expecting to roll up and find another young man who'd got himself in a sticky situation. He'd probably survive the injury, and then come to in the hospital, and get tight-lipped about who had shot him or why, because he wouldn't want to be a snitch. Then me and my boys would dance around in circles for a few weeks, trying to figure out who had pulled the trigger and why, before finally accepting that these kids didn't want our help, and then I'd have to find a way to sleep at night, knowing that some trigger-happy kid with a chip on his shoulder was out there with a gun.

So, I put on my sirens and pressed my foot down on the gas and headed as fast as I could towards the crime scene. I was only a couple of blocks away, so I was the first emergency response vehicle on the scene – and what I saw would stay with me for the rest of my life.

The victim was lying on the sidewalk, bleeding out, and it wasn't a young man in a hooded jumper and sweatpants, decked out in gold pendants and heavy rings. No, this victim was someone altogether different. When I looked at this victim bleeding out fast, I wasn't thinking about what they'd done to get themselves shot, because it was clear to me that this was a true innocent.

No, the young girl of maybe eleven or twelve surely hadn't been caught up in a drug run gone wrong, or asked for a bullet by trespassing on another gang's turf. No, this girl had obviously been caught in some sort of crossfire.

She was a white girl, in a pair of white pants and a pink jumper with sequined butterflies. She had light blonde hair in a mess against the cement, and chipped pink nail polish on the fingers that were clutching at her stomach, where the blood was pouring out. She was white; pale, pale, white. I could already see the life draining out of her when I arrived, and so I wasted no time in dropping to her side while my partner demanded that every damn EMT in the city got down to Western Road – just a block away from the school where she must have been walking home from.

I pressed my own hands down over the wound and applied as much pressure as I could. The young girl was beyond tears or screaming; she was too far gone for that. It was like she already knew that it was too late for her, and I felt her body grow limp under my hands, as her own hands fell down to her sides. Her eyes stayed open, though, and staring at somewhere just beyond my shoulder. I hoped that she was looking far beyond, to somewhere better, where young men with bad tempers and firearms didn't get to decide who lived and who died.

For a while, there was no emotion in me – just adrenalin. Even when the girl went still and cold, I didn't stop trying to save her. My partner pressed his hands down over her stomach so that I could begin to give her CPR until the EMTs arrived. It was the most intense four minutes of my life. Even though the girl wasn't breathing, I was sure that I held her life in my hands. I felt a grave responsibility to keep compressing her chest and breathing into her mouth, in the hope that even though she was so still, and so cold, that somewhere inside of her, life was still holding on.

When the EMTs took over, there was nothing for me to do except call it in. The ambulance loaded up the victim and drove off, sirens blaring, and I was left disoriented and confused next to the puddle of blood where the girl had been. At first, I was in shock; just staring down at the blood on my hands and remembering what it had felt like to feel her warm blood seeping between my fingers, while I tried desperately to keep it in her body.

It took a good few minutes for everything else to register, and, when it did, it hit me like a train, and I felt more than disappointment and frustration at silly boys who got themselves into bad situations. Instead, I felt a deep and wrenching sorrow for the little girl who'd done no wrong, who'd just been in the wrong place at the wrong time.

Her life flashed before my eyes; even though she was a stranger to me. It was her stolen future that I saw – the high school graduation she'd never go to, the first love that would never be, the bride she'd never become, the mother she'd never grow into... In four minutes, I watched the life drain out of a young girl who'd never had a chance to live and I felt my heart genuinely and truly breaking, and it was painful. I thought of my own daughter, and felt this cold dread fill me; because if it wasn't just reckless young men getting shot and killed out there, then it could happen to anyone. My wife could be next. My son. My daughter. Anyone I loved could be the next to be in the wrong place at the wrong time, and that terrified me.

It also made me angry. For years and years I had pounded these pavements, trying to get through to these kids with all the best intentions. And for all the time and effort that I had put into the cause, I had only ever thought about the boys' lives, the boys' potential, the boys' futures... Everything I had done, I had done to make wannabe gangsters put down their guns and pick up a God-damn book to give themselves a better life, because I knew just how easy it was to turn bad in the ghetto. But now... now I could care less about the boys, because what had they cared when they'd not thought twice about pulling a trigger when they saw a little girl walk onto the scene? They'd pulled the trigger anyway, and just hoped they'd get the right guy.

It made me feel hopeless and enraged. While I was out there trying to give these young men better lives and better futures, they were out there taking others' lives and others' futures away. I'd never wanted to be the tyrannical arm of the law tearing young men off the streets and throwing them into jail without taking into consideration the hardships of poverty, racism and violence that they'd had to go through in their lives, but how could I let this continue? This senseless, pointless bloodshed?

My partner came and put his hand on my shoulder. He looked just as shocked as I did, but somehow he managed to speak: "You did all you could, Reg. It's in God's hands now."

I didn't greet Rosie with a kiss. I didn't ask the kids about their days. I didn't sit down for dinner. I went straight on up to the bathroom to shower, and I just hoped the kids wouldn't see the blood on me. I'd washed off as much as I could in the sinks at the precinct, but my uniform was stained. My badge was tarnished red.

Rosie wasn't far behind me as I set the shower running. She stood in the doorway with her arms folded across her chest and ready to lay into me about ignoring my family, when suddenly she caught sight of the bloodstains and her arms fell to her side, and she bit down nervously on her lip.

"What happened today, baby?"

"A girl died."

"How old was she?"

"Eleven or twelve."

"Oh my God. Are you alright? Are you hurt?"

I shook my head. "I'm not hurt… but I'm not alright."

Rosie came and put her arms around me, but I pushed her away, because I didn't want her, also, to be covered in a child's blood. My eyes were brimming with tears, so I kept shutting my eyes tight to hold them back, because Rosie worried enough, without seeing me break down.

I sat down on the edge of the tub while the shower kept running into the tub behind me and the room filled with steam. "I tried so hard to save her, but she didn't make it. She was DOA."

"What happened to her?"

"God knows. It looked like a gunshot to me. I guess she just got in the way of somebody's turf war."

"Oh Reg... I don't know what to say," Rosie confessed.

"There's nothing to say." I let out a long breath, and a slow, sad sigh. "When boys are out for blood, blood is gonna be spilled. It's just so much more of a tragedy when somebody innocent gets in the way. I mean... a little girl, Rosie! What had she ever done to anybody?"

"I know, Reg. It's chaos out there."

"I'm so mad. There are so few of us out there speaking on behalf of those boys. So few to stick up for them and say 'they're not bad people, just born into a bad place'. Then one of them goes and does something like this, and I wonder if I'm on the wrong side of all this. I mean, I'm the one going around saying 'harsh sentences aren't the answer. We need to understand the backgrounds they're coming from; the difficulties they face. Understand. Understand. Understand.' What is there to understand here, huh? I'm speaking up for troubled boys with guns going around shooting little girls walking home from school. It makes my skin crawl that I've been working for them. Do they deserve to be saved?"

"It's just about saving them before it's too late, baby. It's about getting to them before they get to the stage where they pick up a gun – and that's a good cause, baby. That's a fight worth fighting. It's just this time, it was too late."

"It seems like I always get there too late. This year has been hell. Randall. Martel. And now this."

"It's the beat you choose to walk, Reg. You know what it's like out there. You work in a rough, rough neighbourhood."

"I keep thinking about Randall. When he got shot, I thought he was the victim, and I bent over backwards trying to set him straight to save him and give him a better future. Yet, deep down, I know that on another day, he might be the one with a gun in his hand, ready to pull a trigger. Maybe I should just pull him in for the juice he's been slinging and let him sit it out in a cell. Maybe it would save someone else, who really never did no wrong."

"I can't tell you what's right, Reg."

"I try to save kids like Randall, because I *was* a kid like Randall, and I know I'm not evil. I was just young, dumb and stupid. But young, dumb and stupid destroys lives."

"These things are a chain of events Reggie, that start when a kid is born into a poor family in a bad neighbourhood, and that ends when that kid kills someone or does something else horrible like that. It's the chain that needs to break."

CHAPTER TWENTY-SIX

I was taking a few days off the beat while I recovered from the shock of that little girl's death. I'd tried to follow the case as closely as possible in the days that followed, but all that had filtered through so far was the girl's name – Polly – and her age; twelve. She'd died from massive internal bleeding after the bullet had pierced two vital organs.

I just couldn't get her image out of my mind, no matter how hard I tried. I couldn't help thinking how scared she must have been in those final moments, with nobody but strangers around her, as she lay on the ground; so close, but so far from her home.

We were still on the hunt for the gunman, but it was hard work to figure out which gun in a place where a thousand guns had been the one that had fired this particular bullet. It was hard to play the part of detective in a place with so many dark corners to hide in.

There had been no police on that street, and no witnesses – none that had the guts to come forward anyway. Common sense told me that there must have been a shooter, and whoever he'd been aiming at. That meant that somewhere out there was the one that the bullet was meant for, and whoever he was, was keeping his head down and letting the case remain open and unsolved out of fear of having to own up to his own part in this murder.

Murder. That's what it was. Although, it would probably go down as manslaughter or some lesser crime in court; maybe second-degree, as the bullet wasn't meant for Polly. Still, Polly's life had been taken in cold-blood.

I couldn't get my head round the depravity of the shooter. I mean, sure, he'd meant to kill someone else – probably someone much older and much more deserving of a bullet – but he'd missed, and killed an innocent little girl. Yet, his crime didn't stop there. His crime continued when he chose to see the girl drop to the ground and keep on driving. It became more than a drive-by gone wrong, and something much more evil and twisted, when the gunman realised that a little girl was dying, and he chose to drive away to save his own skin, rather than risk a prison sentence to save the life of someone who didn't deserve to die that way.

That's what got me so down about this place. It's just the fact that lives didn't matter here. It didn't matter when they began – nobody made big plans for their kids; like saving for them to go to college, or celebrating their arrival. It was more like a great big panic when another mouth to feed arrived for a family that was already living hand to mouth. Life didn't matter here as those kids aged. They didn't work hard to achieve anything in this world. They didn't dream. They didn't contribute. They just looked around them, saw that everything was bleak and miserable, and decided to live their lives bleak and miserably, too. Life didn't matter any more when it ended. So, a guy jumped from a roof? Big deal; suicide is the one of the leading causes of death for young men – it's just a choice you gotta make sometimes. So, an old man with a big heart breathed his last? So what? Another man with another mission would come along, and maybe make some small difference; maybe not. So what if another young fool died behind bars? Prison was there to make you or break you, and it was survival of the fittest if you got put away. So what if an innocent little girl got caught in the crossfire... when you live in the lion's den, you gotta be prepared to get eaten.

It didn't sit right with me. Not at all. Life should be precious. It should be savoured. It should be nurtured. We should celebrate when a new person is born, and encourage them to grow proud and accomplished and then, when their time came naturally and in good time, we should say goodbye to them with respect and sadness to see one of our own move on.

But, we didn't live like that and we didn't value life here. Everyone just wasted theirs or threw it away, or took someone else's life if they felt they had to. Life was a novelty; a cheap token to be traded or discarded or thrown over your shoulder. Nobody cared about the sanctity and potential of a life. Nobody dreamed big, or lived with passion, or loved with everything in them or reached for the stars. They just slugged along until they gave up or were swallowed up.

I could maybe accept that there were plenty of young men and women out there who had chosen to stay in their slump and view their own potential with no more than a scowl and a shrug; but Polly... well, she'd been just young enough to maybe not realise how hopeless and broken a world she'd been born into. She was a ray of light put out before her time. It was cruel and it was senseless, and I just couldn't figure out how or why it could happen.

So, I did paperwork to make the hours pass while my mind worked it out over and over again and pictured that sweet little girl breathing her last. It made me heart beat faster as that deep and passionate calling inside of me screamed for me to hear it – only, I couldn't quite understand what it was saying any more. There was a voice inside me screaming, 'save them! Save them!'. Only, I couldn't figure out who was the victim anymore – the innocent young girl who was shot down on her way home from school, or a young man who'd only pulled the trigger because his world was so small and closed in, and his life so empty and broken, that those stupid, meaningless, petty street grudges seemed to him to be worth killing and dying for.

My endless administration was interrupted by a familiar presence in front of my desk. I looked up to see Mr Branch – Peter – standing in front of me. I stood up and smiled, before I realised that Peter wasn't smiling. In fact, he looked completely broken; standing there with his eyes red and puffy, his hair thinner than before, his skin pale and his spectacles in his hands, so that he could rub his tired, swollen eyes again. His voice was quiet when he spoke.

"Reggie. It's good to see you."

"Mr Branch, you look terrible. What's happened?"

Peter's lip quivered and he gestured towards the empty chair in front of my desk to ask if he could sit. I nodded quickly, and sat back down with him.

"I'm sorry, Reggie. I thought you must have known."

"Known what?"

"Who she was?"

"Who?"

"Polly."

"The girl that died?"

"Yes, the girl that... died. Polly was my daughter."

The news hit me like a tonne of bricks, and for a moment I was too stunned to reply. What had already been a tragedy burning a hole inside my heart, now turned into an emotional wildfire inside of me, because the stranger child that had died in my arms had not been so much of a stranger after all.

"Peter, I'm so sorry. The boss has been sheltering me from the case. I was so shook up... I just didn't know. I'm so sorry."

Peter just looked down at his lap and blinked rapidly to hold back tears. He took a deep breath to calm himself. "I was told that you were the one who was there with her. I just wanted to thank you for trying... I know how hard you tried."

He was here to thank me, but it hurt so damned much to hear it. He was thanking me for failing him and his little girl. And it wasn't the first time I'd let a friend's child get shot either... What was wrong with me? I was no protector for these kids. I was no good at all.

"I don't know what to say, Peter. You know we're doing everything we can here, right?"

Peter simply shrugged, like he was tired and like he'd given up. "Even if you find them, it won't bring her back."

"It would be justice for you and Andrea."

"There is no justice in this place, Reggie. You know that. It's just an endless cycle that continues on and on. As long as there are people shooting, there are people getting shot. One day you're on one side of the gun, the next you're on the other. There is no justice; just a tide we all get pulled in by – in and out – just hoping we're not the next to get swept away."

"We will find the ones responsible. I promise. And we'll put them away, so that you can sleep at night."

Peter laughed scornfully; tearfully. "I'll never sleep again. Put one gunman away and another will step up to take his place. The only way to break the cycle is education, perseverance, opportunities and understanding."

"How can you forgive something like this?"

"Forgive?" Peter spat. "I will never forgive the ones who did this, and the ones out there hiding in the shadows now. My daughter is gone, and she died in a violent and terrible way. No father should have to outlive his little girl. No father should have to identify her body, and then pick out a coffin. I will never forgive, and I will never forget – but I will fight. I will fight until the bitter end, because if somebody doesn't push back against the depravity and the suffering, then depravity and suffering will be all there is. It's not about punishing this person or that person that assaults, or steals or kills, but about breaking down the system that makes them do it. Trust me, Reggie – I do not feel sympathy for the ones who did this. They can rot in hell for what they've done. But I will do everything in me to stop it happening again. That means digging down deep until I can find some compassion and understanding for the rest of them out there, thinking about drawing a gun. I'm on a mission to get to them and show them I understand, before they strike out because they think nobody's listening. All of this is about pride. Stupid, stupid pride. And what drives this pride; this gang loyalty; this need to be respected and feared? Insecurity. And why are they insecure? Because they've got nothing. There's nothing to make them feel empowered or courageous or big. So they go out killing and shooting and everything else, because it feels a lot like power, and a lot like courage; and when everyone's afraid of them, it makes them feel big."

"Everyone talks about the cycle, about the chain. They're talking about poverty and violence and a lack of opportunity. But what can be done, Peter? How do we stop it?"

"Whatever the problem-education is always part of the solution. Funding. Youth programmes. Training. Apprenticeships. Building. Bus routes. Jesus, Reggie – I don't care. Anything and everything that says 'you are not forgotten and you are not less than anybody else on this damned earth'. If they believed that – truly believed that – then, BOOM. There goes the insecurity. No more need to be revered and feared by everyone else, because maybe they'd have some damned self-respect, and bigger ambitions than being the toughest thug in their gang."

"You're right, Peter. And you've got my support. I'll do whatever I can to help you."

"You can start by coming back into the school. You used to do talks for me, and then you disappeared." Peter looked at me earnestly with big, round, desperate eyes. "I don't know if what we're doing there does any good or makes any difference – but I've got to believe. I need something to hold onto. Now more than ever. Polly's gone, but there's a thousand other Pollys out there, and any one of them could be next. Prevention is better than cure, Reggie. It's not about cleaning up the streets after the gangs and criminals have made a mess. It's about making streets that people don't want to mess up. It's about building community, and building hope. It's a cycle, Reg, but in a way that gives me hope, because it means that after this generation of kids, another will come and another and then another – which means that we will never run out of chances to try again. And I believe – deep down in the core of me, I believe – that if we, as a community, as a nation, as individuals – keep on trying and trying and trying, that one day we'll break through, and this place can heal, and the chain will be broken. We've got to make a community that does right by its citizens. I mean, every time someone here does good, they leave – because good doesn't last in this neighbourhood. We don't want the good to leave and the bad to fester. Let's heal this place from the inside out."

"I can't believe how fired up you sound after everything that's happened. After losing Polly. I haven't been able to sleep. I've lost my drive. I've lost my rhythm. I don't know what's up and what's down anymore. I can't figure out where to begin when everything seems so screwed up."

"I know," Peter said. "When I first found out about Polly, all I wanted to do was go out for blood, and maybe burn that school to the ground so that I would never have to go back and face it all again – a school hall filled with kids destined to kill, and kids destined to die, and so many destined to fall somewhere in-between; never really living. I didn't want to go back. I hate that other parents' kids are still kicking and breathing when my little girl..." Peter drew in a deep breath that was so sharp I could almost feel his pain. He let out a long, sorrowful breath. "I keep telling myself that I raised Polly with values. Those values were that hard work and determination were enough to overcome any obstacles. I taught her that we had to believe in ourselves, and we had to believe that change and growth were possible. If I don't live up to that now, then everything I taught her was a lie. I have to work hard now, and be determined and believe that something good can come from this tragedy. That's why I'm starting the Polly Foundation."

"The Polly Foundation?"

"I'm going to go out into the world and talk about her. Tell her story. Make people think about their actions and who they just might end up hurting. I'm going to raise money to sponsor kids' educations in her name and for her sake. I'm going to set up programmes for the youth in this city – open to all. I'm going to send a message loud and clear: if you want to be better, then I'm throwing open my doors. Let's all be better. I'm going to get others to tell their stories. From all sides – the mothers whose sons they only see once a month in a prison visiting ward; the young men who took a life and can't forgive themselves for what they've done; the friends and families of young people who've died in gang shootings. I'm going to paint a picture from all angles that tells people that *this is not the way*. And it's going to be real, and personal and straight to the point. Maybe it'll make them think twice, and maybe it won't. All I know is that I've got to keep talking as loud and as to many people as I can, until that message is heard in every deepest, darkest corner of this neighbourhood. I don't know if it'll do any good. I don't know if it'll make a difference, but at least I'll have tried to make a difference. That's all we can do, Reggie: try."

CHAPTER TWENTY-SEVEN

Here I was again, at Harold Washington High School to talk to the kids again. For a long time now, I'd been feeling disillusioned about what I was doing, and whether anybody was really hearing what I had to say, but today it wasn't about me and my message alone. Today I was here to support Peter as he introduced the Polly Foundation for the first time to his own students.

I stood in that school hall once again and looked out over the faces of students who'd heard me speak before. A few of the faces I recognised – Jey was the son of Marla; a woman I'd brought in more than once for public intoxication. Poor kid. He'd had a tough time. There was Bret; he'd been into the station more than once for drugs, and next to him Eddie, who'd been brought in for worse. Ella was in the crowd. She'd been caught buying drugs, and promising sexual favours – she was only seventeen.

It made me sad to realise that I only knew any of these kids because they'd run into hard times or had already started down the wrong path. If there were kids in here striving to do better, or staying out of trouble, then I wouldn't know of them. I wondered how many in the stands would fit the latter description. How many of these kids were staying straight?

The hall was set up for the presentation with two giant boards on stands that bore the image of Polly's grinning face – and that was all. I looked around and could see a few students staring curiously at that picture, wondering who she was. I wondered what they'd think when they were told her story.

The students had noticed me standing on the side-lines. I could see some of them rolling their eyes, grinning and getting distracted before the assembly had even begun, because they didn't want to hear anymore from me. Except, I wasn't the one starting this conversation.

Mr Branch stepped forward. God knows how he was back in his role already, only three weeks after Polly had died. I'm sure that some of the students had heard about his daughter's death, but maybe not, as these stories weren't uncommon in the papers and on the news around here, so they'd probably not even paid attention to one more.

Peter stepped up to the mic in the centre of the hall and called the students to attention.

"Listen up, everyone. Listen up."

Some of the more respectful students quietened down, but some of them kept on chattering.

"I said *listen!*" Peter's voice was louder this time, and sharp, and it must have surprised the students to hear their usually mild-mannered principal raise his voice. A hush fell. Peter took a moment to let the intensity build – or maybe just to gain control of his own emotions, as everything he was about to say was personal and raw. He pointed to the picture of Polly.

"This is Polly. Now, most of you will have no idea who this girl is, but I guarantee that many of you will have met her. You might have seen her skipping around on parents' evening, or sitting in the bleachers at one of our football games. You might have walked past her on the street, or sat nearby her in a diner. She was one of you, you see. She was born in this community and she lived here." He paused. "And she died here."

The silence amongst the students became more sombre when they realised where this speech was going, and I was grateful for the fact that they seemed to have at least some respect for the death of Polly. Mr Branch continued.

"Something else you might not know about this girl – Polly – is that she was my daughter. Three weeks ago she died because someone out there with a gun needed to get his point across. Except, he didn't shoot the one he meant to kill – he shot Polly."

"Polly was twelve years old. She wanted to be a doctor. She was good at Math. She liked to sing. Her dream in life was to grow up and to help people, but that will never happen now, because she'll never grow up."

"Now, as I'm sure you can all imagine, the last thing that I wanted to do at this time was to come back here and carry on working like nothing had ever happened – like my family and my life hadn't been torn apart, but I am an educator, and there is a lesson to be learned here."

"The lesson is that sometimes there is no going back. Sometimes it is just too late. Sometimes the things you are trying to prove just end up backfiring and hurting somebody innocent. In this community, ladies and gentlemen, we have a serious problem with violence. We have a serious problem with firearms. And we have a serious problem in the attitudes of the people living here. We don't value our lives. Not our own, and not each other's."

"I have watched over for many years as many of you come to this place of learning to do nothing more than smoke and hang out with your friends. Meanwhile you're not engaged in your learning, you ignore your teachers and don't bother doing your assignments, and have fights in the cafteria. These will all seem like trivial things to you when we're living in a place where people are killing and dying every day, but these trivial things matter. Why? Because the fact that you will come to school just to fight and hang out is proof that you don't care about your own lives. Every day that you ignore your teachers and use the pages of your books as papers for your smokes, you're wasting your own opportunities. And then you'll grow bitter and tell the world and yourself that you were never given an opportunity."

Mr Branch paused dramatically and then shrugged sadly. "As I see it, every one of you has an opportunity to invest in yourself and your own future, but you choose not to. It's not cool to buckle down and study. There's no honour in it. There's no clout."

Peter pointed to the picture of Polly once again and looked at the faces of his students sternly. "Let me tell you: there is no honour in *this*. There is no honour in a twelve-year-girl being shot down on her way home from school. Yet, every day, this is the choice I see people making. They choose to go out on a mission to spill blood, rather than to roll up their sleeves and get stuck into making this this a better place."

"I find myself at a loss as to what to say to you that hasn't been said before. You have all been born into difficult and challenging circumstances. Some of you have problems to deal with that children shouldn't have to endure. We live in an challenging environment, ladies and gentlemen; an environment where there is little hope. And all of you accept this."

"You don't think that you accept this, but you do. You believe that joining gangs, getting hold of a gun, slinging drugs, fighting, killing, committing crimes… you believe that all these things are acts of rebellion which send the message: I am not satisfied with this life."

"Let me tell you: you're not sending the message you think that you are. The message you are actually sending is that you *are* satisfied with what we have here. You are showing that you are satisfied with violence and crime and poverty, because you choose to participate in it. You choose to expand it. You choose to squash out the good and the benign, and to build on the hateful and vengeful. You're born with a chip on your shoulder, and are happy to carry that the rest of your lives. None of you have the maturity or the foresight to shrug it off and think about what we could have if we all made the choice, *today*, to turn our backs on what was given to us, and take instead, what we could have."

"I'm not talking about gang glory and street cred. I'm talking about building foundations for your lives to build truly good things. I'm talking about stable, loving home lives and fulfilling, rewarding careers. All of you can have these things, but change comes from within. Change must come from within. Change must come from within each of us."

"I've seen young men and women who are happy to do terrible things to 'earn' respect. They will kill for it. They will commit crimes for it. They will betray trust for it. They will do enormous acts to earn their place in the hierarchy of the street. These young men and women will demonstrate determination and stamina to do these terrible things for all the wrong reasons. Yet, these same young men and women will tell us that it is too hard to graduate. That it is too hard to get a job. That it is too hard to raise their children." Peter shrugged sorrowfully. "Personally, I don't buy that."

He sighed heavily and looked over at his daughter's picture sadly and meaningfully. "Remember how this speech started today when you're tempted to roll your eyes and think that I don't know your story and this doesn't apply to you. Let me tell you something – this speech didn't apply to her. Polly didn't need to be told not to carry a gun. She did not contribute to the sad and terrible things taking place here. She had less reason than any of you to ever believe that something bad would happen to her or that she would wind up dead. Her mother and I had no reason to believe that we would have to bury our little girl and shut her bedroom door forever because it hurts too much to look inside at her empty bed and untouched things. This speech was not for her – yet, here we are. This speech is all about her. I think the point I'm trying to make, ladies and gentlemen, is that nobody is immune to the sickness that resides here. But, every one of you holds the key to the cure. The key is self-realisation, education and determined change. You must realise that if you are not part of the solution, you are part of the problem. If you are fighting, or stealing or slinging drugs or committing crimes, you are not standing up and protesting – you are giving in and letting all those things you hate drag on forever. So, each of you must be determined to protest in the only way that counts; the only way that will make a difference. You must fight what is bad with what is good. Fight low graduation rates and unemployment by studying hard and earning those jobs. I promise you that it won't take long – a generation or two – before businesses arise from nothing because you have created them, and when the next set of kids graduate – lo and behold; there are jobs waiting for them, so the cycle ends. Fight the low expectations, by expecting better from yourself. Don't take the drugs. Don't drink yourself into a stupor so that you do things you regret. Ladies and gentlemen, *there is so much you can do.* You are not powerless. You are not ineffective. You have huge potential and immense opportunity, but you have to make the choice. As always, our assembly boils down to what it always does – choices."

Peter looked over at me and I knew that it was my turn to speak. I stepped forward and addressed the students. "You all recognise me. I've been here before to talk to you about choices. It's very sad that I come back here to talk to you about choices again because someone made a bad one, and now a girl is dead. And I know that this story is not unfamiliar to you. Nearly everybody in this room will have lost someone before their time, due to the issues that Mr Branch was talking about – poverty, violence and low expectations. Some of you have had family members – parents, even – die from drugs or violence. Some of you have lost loved ones to gun crime – brothers, and sisters. Some of you may not have had to attend a funeral yet, but you've still lost people close to you – they're in prison now."

I saw some of the kids start to look genuinely upset, because now I was speaking to their own experiences. I carried on. "I lost one of my best friends when he died in prison. It's a story I tell often, and I know many of you have heard it. More recently, I lost a cousin to a fatal shooting – it was a case of wrong place, wrong time. He was from out of town, just visiting. He'd done nothing to nobody. Now I am called upon again because the daughter of a good friend – your principal, Mr Branch – has died the same way. What I am saying is that we are all affected by these issues, so why is there so much division between us? Why do we form gangs and strike out against each other? Why do we convince ourselves that our pain is unique and nobody understands? Let me tell you: your pain is real, but it is not unique. And that is wrong. It is so, so wrong. If a kid came to me grieving because a loved one had been shot down or put away in prison, and I could say it was one-off; trust me, that would be a good day. But these things are not one-offs. They happen all the time. They happen to the best of us. They happen to the worst of us."

"To drive that home, let me give you a breakdown of some of the worst cases that our station dealt with this month. Female, 24, drug overdose. Male, 18, fatal shooting. Male, 18, fatal stabbing. Female, 19, taken in for child abuse. Female, 17, possession of heroin. Male, 28, hit-and-run – 8-year old victim in critical condition. Female, 46, theft. Males, 16, 18, and 17 – armed robbery; three injured." I paused for effect and then continued. "If I am here too often and you're getting sick of me, it's because there is still so much left to say. The day the violence stops is the day I stop interrupting your lives to give speeches. So, I echo what Mr Branch has to say to you all – protest in the right way; by being different, not by being the same. There is no rebellion, no statement, and no protest in crime and violence. You are not telling people that you are unhappy with your life, you're telling them that you are willingly a part of it. If you want to break the system you hate, you have to step outside of it. Do not be cog in the machine that forms the ghetto."

"I know many of us don't like that word. Ghetto. Do you know what the dictionary definition of a ghetto is? It is a slum area, inhabited predominately by a minority group and affected by hardships caused by economic and social restrictions." I held up my hands as if to challenge anybody to dispute that definition. "I hate to say it, but that's what we have here. We graffiti and vandalise our buildings; we have trap houses; we smash in their windows. We build a slum to live in. We are affected by hardships; every one of us. A lot of us struggle with money issues. We struggle with drug issues. We struggle with the effect that prison has had on us and our families. There are economic and social restrictions on us – a lack of jobs, poor infrastructure, troubled schools, racism, crime. And many of us are from a minority background. By definition, we cannot deny our situations. We are facing disadvantage and hardship – so let's break the definition. Don't vandalise your city; take pride in it. Take part in the programs that renovate and restore our buildings; that create parks and sports grounds and then respect the work that is done.

Overcome the issues in your own lives by learning from the mistakes of those around you, rather than repeating them. Work hard. Study. Find employment. Stay on the straight and narrow. Do this and the economic and social restrictions will fade away. Create your own prosperity, ladies and gentlemen. Don't fall into the definition of a label you despise."

"To help you, Mr Branch and I are proud to announce the collaboration of our station, Family Matters and his charity – the Polly Foundation – in supporting our youth. In the coming weeks and months, we will be promoting many new initiatives such as work programs, mentorships, community service, funding programs and open counselling. There will be an opportunity for every one of you, if you choose to take it. I ask you to seriously think about everything that has been said here today, and to make the choice to participate. The more of us, the better. Let's be united. Let's show some of that determination and stamina we're known for, and let's put it to good use. The next time I come here, I don't want to have to be reeling off a list of tragedies to try and get through to you. Hear me now – I beg you. Because, if we can learn anything from the tragedy of Polly's death, it's that nothing can be fixed once it's already too late. Don't wait until it's too late to act. The time is now."

CHAPTER TWENTY-EIGHT

I t was only by chance that I caught sight of Randall under that same bridge I'd found him when I'd last gone looking for him, but I thought it was as good a time as any to give getting through to him another shot. Since Polly had been murdered, I'd found a new resolve and a new determination in myself. Some of that sense of calling was coming back and I was starting to piece together exactly what fight I was fighting once again. It was still not quite clear whose side I was on, or who I should be helping, because I could see the pain on both sides, but I was starting to develop a sense that my mission was something like this: prevent suffering as much as you can in any way you can, and when you get there too late, accept that picking up the pieces is still a worthy cause.

Hmm, it needed some work, but it was helping to try and determine my cause again. It used to be solely about helping the young men before they got too far gone, but my cause had become bigger than that now. I felt like Batman in Gotham – my cause was to save the whole damned town. But I was just one man.

Randall wasn't happy to see me, but he didn't move away either. He just rolled his eyes in his typical Smooth fashion and gave me a withering glare.

"Nice to see you too," I greeted him. "What's that you're smoking, Randall? It smells like something I could take you in for."

"So, that I can die in prison too? You want to get to me just like you did my Dad?"

Randall was so bitter, and I didn't really understand it. I'd spent a long time thinking about Leo over the years and how he'd died, and I was getting closer to believing that his death hadn't been entirely my fault. There had been so many factors at play leading up to our arrest and Leo's death in prison, and I'd only been one of them. I tried to explain this to Randall.

"You weren't there for the assembly at school the other day," I said, "but I wish you had've been. It might've meant something to you."

"I doubt it."

"It was about choices, and about making statements. About the right way to protest at a shit life."

"Let me guess? I should join the volunteer squad and go around picking up trash to make the world sunshiney-sweet again."

"Something like that." I sighed. Randall was determined to hate me; to blame me, and that made it very difficult to be able to explain anything to him at all. "The point we were trying to make is that we were all born into the hood, but the people have to change before the place can change."

"You expect a lot from people who never had nothing to start with."

"Yeah, Randall. I do. I do expect a lot from you kids. And is that a bad thing? Everybody wants change to come, but nobody wants to be held accountable for what's causing all this trouble in the hood. Sure, things were messed up here before any of us came along, but if we make no effort to leave it a little better than we found it, then we're as much to blame as our parents and the ones who came before them. There has to be a generation that says 'enough is enough'. Tell me, Randall – are you gonna be a part of that generation?"

He rolled his eyes with even more exaggeration and stamped the rest of his blunt out on the ground. "You think your speeches are much better than they are, Reg. All you do is sound like a preacher."

"I'm learning to be OK with that. At least I'm not some old record, spouting the same self-pitying shit that has been played a thousand times before. Sound like anyone you know?"

"Is that what you wanted to talk to me about, Reg? Just needed another chance to make your point, huh? What is your point, anyway?"

"You're heading down a dangerous path." I told him seriously. "Do you even know half the shit that Butch is into?"

"Yeah, I'd heard you'd spoke to Cody," Randall replied with heavy disapproval in his voice. "Is it your personal mission to ruin my life?"

"I'm trying to help."

"You're making people think that I'm a rat. I mean, what are people gonna think when a cop has got a special interest in someone they roll with? He wants to be all buddy-buddy with him? If I get shot again, it's probably gonna be on you."

"Wow. You're real desperate to have someone to blame, ain't ya? If you get shot again, you'll want to believe that it was my fault for speaking to Cody, but you won't think for one second that maybe it'd be your fault for rolling with someone who likes guns so much and is happy to point one at a so-called 'friend'. You wouldn't like to think you should take any blame for that at all – just like you don't think your Dad had anything to answer for with how he died."

"Don't you dare speak about my Dad, Reg – not after what you did."

"What did I do, Randall? Look at yourself – you're walking in his very footsteps. You're hanging with a group of boys who are too happy to go looking for trouble. If you go out on a drug deal with the two of them – like I went out to burgle with Leo and Winston – and the three of you get picked up, and then one of you dies in prison; whose fault is it? The one who arranged the deal? His alone? Or have you all got to question why you went along with it? That's where you're heading, Randall. You're heading to a big deal gone wrong and death or prison time. You could have walked away months ago. You could walk away now. But you won't. You won't stop until it's all too late."

"What would you have me do? Say, 'sorry, guys; can't tonight – I've got a book report to do'?"

"And what is wrong with that apart from the fact that you don't want to look like a punk in front of them? Trust me, you'd be glad you were a punk when they're inside and you've got a nice house with a wife and kids, doing well for yourself."

"It ain't gonna happen like that, though, is it? I ain't got the smarts, Reggie. It's not about 'choices', like you like to say. Some things are decided for us, and you gotta roll with them that way."

"Bullshit, Randall. For God's sake, step up and take some responsibility for your own life! If you end up in prison, that'll be on you. You'll be blaming your Dad 'cause he's not here, and your Mom 'cause she's got her drug issues, and your Grandma 'cause she didn't pander to you and tell you that you were an angel, and me 'cause I spoke to Cody… and you'll forget all the months that we've all been telling you that you're heading for disaster and that we've done everything we can to pull you back from the edge. Sure, Randall, you've had some tough times in your life; but one day you gotta get to an age where you realise that you can either let the excuse of a bad childhood rule you forever, or you can recognise that now you're a man and you make your own decisions. What's it gonna be?"

Randall sighed impatiently. "Another great speech, Reggie. You rehearse that one? Sounds like you spent ages sitting in your cosy little house thinking that one up. Great job."

"Sarcasm won't save you."

"And neither will you."

"I think I might just have to accept that. I'm running out of ideas to try and help you out."

"Thank God – enough already."

I gave a little shrug. "Fine then, Randall. Have it your way. I won't interfere in your life no more. I'll take a step back. If you need me, you know where I am. Let's just hope when we next meet, it's not because I'm leading you to a cell, or zipping up a body bag."

"I'm hoping we don't meet again, Reg."

I held up my hands submissively. I had to let this go now. Randall was not really a kid no more. He'd heard everything me and everyone else had to say, and it wasn't enough for him. He'd been shot, and it hadn't made the message stick. He'd lost his Dad to prison violence, and that wasn't enough to make him think twice. He'd had every shock in the book to snap him out of it, and enough tough love for a dozen kids, but it just wasn't what he wanted to hear. He didn't want to change. So be it.

There had to be a point where I drew the line for my own sanity. I had a wife and kids at home who hardly ever saw me and were deeply affected when I brought the job home; so, I had to leave my failures behind at the end of the day. I had to brush my hands clean of Randall and his stubbornness and accept that I clocked out at eight.

It was a hard choice to make, and not one that came naturally to me, but I was learning that balance in my own life mattered, because I was one overtime shift away from a mental breakdown, and if I let that happen, then I'd lose everything that I'd worked for in my own life. So, today, I had to leave Randall to smoke his weed under a bridge and convince himself that that was the best he could do and exactly what he wanted. I had to let him stay angry at the world and at me. And I had to go home and tell my wife and kids I loved them.

CHAPTER TWENTY-NINE

I had kept my promise and stayed away from Randall since we'd last spoken. I'd not pulled in Cody or Butch for any more secret chats and I'd not been round to Flo's to talk to her any more about her wayward grandson. Still, it wasn't long before I felt I had reason to see Flo, after I heard through the grapevine that she'd been taken into hospital after the police had been called to the scene of an elderly women wandering aimlessly in front of traffic.

I can't say that I was surprised to hear about it. There were odd things that I'd noticed in Flo's behaviour in the months that I had known her that I'd put down to stress and old age. One particular example that sticks in mind happened a few weeks back, when I asked Flo how she had been keeping and she began to tell me about conversations she'd had with her husband that day... her husband who had died years earlier.

I'd mentioned my concerns to Shannon, but she'd not wanted to hear them – and I knew why. I had my own suspicions about Shannon, too. She'd seemed kinda out of it the last few times I'd seen her, which made me think that maybe she wasn't as clean and sober as she'd like me to believe.

I went to see Flo in the hospital when I heard the news. She'd gotten a lot worse since I'd last met with her to speak about Randall. I tried to speak with her, and although her words were clear and she could hold a conversation, her memory was warped, like she was living in a different timeline to the rest of us. She was talking about things that happened years ago as if they'd happened today, and things that had happened recently she reacted to as if she was hearing of them for the first time.

"I'm sorry I haven't seen you lately, Flo," I told her as I sat at her hospital bedside. "Once the whole Randall situation cooled down, life just got hectic in other ways again. I should've come by to say hi."

"Randall? What's wrong with Randall?"

"Don't you remember, Flo? He's running with a bad crowd."

"Well, Shannon's taken him away from all that."

"Randall has been living with you."

"No, no. With Leo gone, Shannon wasn't sticking around. Her and the baby are gone."

I frowned. Flo seemed to be stuck in the past, thinking that Randall was still a newborn and living with Shannon away from this town. I wondered how much help Flo could really be in my next line of enquiry.

"Flo, do you know where Randall is? I need to get in touch with him to find out what he's gonna do while you're in hospital."

Flo looked over my shoulder to the nurse behind me and called out to her agitatedly. "Do you know who this man is? Can you get him out of here? I'm trying to read."

The nurse gave me a sympathetic glance and I shook my head in response, but stood to leave. "Not to worry, ma'am," I said to Flo, "I'm leaving now."

I left the hospital wondering what my next move should be. Randall was young enough that I felt he shouldn't be home alone while his grandmother was in hospital, but old enough that I wondered how much authority I could really assert. I wasn't used to dealing in family issues like this – that was more a line of social work. I didn't want Randall unsupervised with the path he was on, but the only person left in his life to watch over him was Shannon, and she wasn't the best role model for a troubled kid.

I went back to the precinct to talk it over with Winston, who was in the break room drinking a coffee and reading the finance section of the newspaper. I sat down at his table with him and he could tell straight away that I wanted to talk.

"I'm on break, Reggie. Can it wait?"

"It's about Randall."

Winston sighed and placed down his coffee mug on the table, sat back and gestured for me to continue. "Tell me, then."

"Flo's in hospital."

"Is she alright?"

"She's undergoing assessment, but no, I don't think she's alright."

"What's wrong with her?"

"I'm guessing Alzheimer's."

"What makes you think that?"

"She's confused. Very confused. Picked up wandering around in traffic. Thinks Randall's a baby and off with Shannon somewhere."

Winston frowned. "It could be any number of things, Reg. People's medication can make them act loopy. I know my Nana was acting all kinds of strange when she had a kidney infection. It's just like you to go into a panic. Let the doctors do their jobs. A course of antibiotics and she may well be back to her proper senses."

"Well, I hope you're right Winston, but we need to think about what we're going to do about Randall if she's not OK."

"Well, what do you think would happen?" Winston asked me seriously. "I know a lot of kids living with parents with alcohol problems, drug problems, disabilities... If he was living with her with Alzheimer's, it wouldn't be ideal, but the only alternative is a foster placement, and he's at an age where I think that would do more damage than living with a grandmother who needs some care. Besides, if Flo's unwell, he's always got Shannon."

"He went to live with Flo because Shannon was trying to kick her habits and get him out of harm's way. Only thing is, I think Shannon's off the rails."

"Why d'you think that?"

"I've seen enough people on drugs to know what it looks like."

"Sure. OK. Still, what do you want to happen, Reg? Our support system is busting at the seams with kids a lot younger and in a lot more need that Randall. There's no use throwing him in with them when he's got a perfectly good roof over his head with Flo. We'll just keep an eye on him, get social services involved to pop in now and then... what's the issue?"

"The issue? My issue is that that's the best we're going to do for him. Leave him with an unstable guardian and a drug addict mother."

Winston gave me a sympathetic look, but shrugged. "I hear you, Reggie, I do. But, what do you want me to do? Pull out a stable, wealthy family looking for a troubled sixteen-year-old to care for out of thin air? Even if we found somewhere for Randall to go, you know as well as me that he wouldn't go there. He's in no worse a situation then we were when we were kids."

"My point exactly. Look how we ended up."

"Call Gina, Reggie. She's the one who knows about these sort of things. She'll tell you what your options are, but I really don't think you're gonna get far with this. Randall is a young man now, not a kid. As long as he's being provided with his basic needs, I think the state's gonna be satisfied."

"And what about the guidance and support huh? What about the kick up the ass he needs to go to school and stay out of trouble?"

"Reg, you know and I know that Randall ain't gonna respond to that from nobody. We've all tried. My advice is to just keep an eye on him, like you always do, but leave it at that. Get in touch with Gina, so she can make sure the right people know about his situation, and that's that."

"Somebody needs to do more for him."

"Well, I don't want him in my house with my kids. You want him in your house with yours?"

I felt a sick sense of guilt turning in my stomach, because, no, I didn't want Randall in my house. As much as I spouted that somebody had to do right by him and keep an eye on him and provide for him, the thought of him bringing all his issues and danger to my doorstep was not something I could come to terms with. Randall had already got himself stabbed once – what if I brought him into my home and his enemies followed? What if my son or daughter became another Polly? No, it couldn't be done.

"Fine. I'll speak to Gina."

"Good," Winston nodded. "Look, Reg, you've got nothing to feel guilty over. You've done more than most would already. You talk to these kids endlessly about choices and you've gotta accept that if Randall spirals out of control because Flo isn't around, then that's on him. He knows where we are if he needs us."

"Randall's sixteen years old," I replied. "He's got a grandmother who's probably got Alzheimer's, a dead father, and a drunk mother on drugs. He turns to other troubled young people because they're the only friends he's got, yet, if he gets in trouble, we're gonna say 'it's on him'? It doesn't sit easy with me, Winston. Yeah, the kid will make his choices, but I can't believe that the bad ones we'll be wholly on him. He's a victim of circumstance."

"Every one of us in this town is a victim of circumstance. You were a victim of circumstance. I was a victim of circumstance. Leo was a victim of circumstance. Yet, you and me are here and alive and kicking and working and earning and taking care of our families because we knew when to say enough was enough, grow up and take responsibility – and we were no older when we made that choice than Randall is now. You've done all you can. You've warned him and tried to educate him. You've intervened. You've pulled strings. You've watched out for him. That is a hell of a load more care and attention than most of these kids have. Yeah, it's a harsh world out there, and yeah, I feel sorry for him, but the choice he's gotta make now is the same choice every one of us has to make at his age – go down with the ship, or swim to the shore."

I took Rosie out for a nice dinner, as it had been a long time since we'd last been on a date. Winston's niece was babysitting the kids for us. We'd had a nice evening so far. Rosie looked incredible in a blue dress and heels, with the diamond necklace I'd bought for her on our fifth wedding anniversary around her neck. She looked even more beautiful than the day I'd met her. I'd tried so hard to avoid talking about work or the things that were on my mind while we were getting some time away from it all, but after a couple of hours of peaceful conversation, Rosie was the one to bring the conversation back to things I was thinking about.

"How's Flo doing?"

"She's back home, but they're putting a care plan into place for her. I was right. Alzheimer's."

"Poor Flo. Poor Randall. How's his mum doing?"

"Not great. She's back on the bottle."

Rosie sighed heavily. "It's strange to think that all these things happen right on our doorsteps. Everyone's got things going on behind closed doors, haven't they?"

"They sure do."

"It makes me glad that we've found the peace we have. You know, I still dream sometimes about moving away to the country."

"Neither of us would find work in the country."

"You don't think so? See, I could see you settling down as a humble cop in a small town, and I'd go into teaching. The kids could go to a nice school, and we'd all go for picnics at the weekend. I think it would be nice."

"I bet it would be."

Rosie sighed and smiled sadly. "But you'd never be able to get your community off your mind, so you wouldn't enjoy that country life, would you?"

"I'd try – for you."

"I'd never make you give it all up, Reggie. It drives me mad, and I hate you for it sometimes, but I love you much more."

"How'd I get so lucky to meet a woman like you?"

"One of the reasons I fell in love with you was because you genuinely cared about your town and the people in it. So few people in this world genuinely care about anything, let alone do everything they can to follow their cause and make the world better. You were, and still are, just too special to let go. Sometimes I want to be mad at you for putting me second place all the time, but then I think to myself that the causes you fight for are a worthy first place.

You're doing good with your life, and I would never take that away from you."

"Not so long ago I thought you were doubting the good I was doing."

"Not so long ago I thought you were too."

"I was doubting, but I'm getting back on track now. It's an exhausting game, Rosie, but it's the one I was born to play."

CHAPTER THIRTY

I was called in to speak with Captain Russell. She was the woman I respected most in this world apart from Rosie. Like all of us, she'd started with nothing in the hood. Her father had been a back-street arms dealer, and her mother had a lot of other men in her life. Captain Russell – Sandra, to her inner circle – had had a hard and challenging childhood without a single positive influence in her life. But, she had worked to overcome her personal challenges and had strived to defeat them. She'd kept her head down in school and studied hard. She'd joined the police force aged eighteen and quickly flown up the ranks to become the youngest captain our force had ever had. She was forty-two now and a ferocious and straight-talking woman, but I liked her a lot. Although she was fast-talking and stern to the public eye, I knew that she had a heart of gold and a lot of sincerity in her. I felt for her, though, because she always had to make the tough calls around here, and, as the face of the department, she dealt with a lot of grief from the neighbourhood. They'd demand to know what the hell we were doing with our time, and it was hard to watch when Captain Russell was the most dedicated woman I'd ever met.

I didn't get called into her office very often. It only usually happened when there was a reason to debrief after a critical incident or if something was happening in our ranks. Today, it seemed, it was both.

I knocked respectfully on the door and waited until I was called in to enter. Sandra was standing behind her desk looking out the window at the basketball courts that could be seen just beyond the next row of buildings. She turned around, gave me a tired but welcoming smile.

She was a plain-looking woman, but not unattractive. She was dark-skinned and steely-eyed with lips that were always closely drawn together as though she was resisting the urge to bark orders or tell secrets. She always wore her hair drawn back in a very tight bun on the back of her head and her uniform was always meticulously ironed and tucked in. Today she was wearing a navy pant suit with a white shirt and small heels. She looked fierce. I waited until she gestured for me to sit down and then took a seat by her desk. She then sat down on the opposite side of the desk, and, just as she always did, got straight down to business.

"JJ got shot last night," she told me. "He was off-duty but a con he'd arrested years ago recognised him and took his shot. I guess there was some bad feeling there after a five-year stint in the slammer."

"Oh shit," I gasped. "Is JJ OK?"

"Wounded, but he'll survive," Sandra told me. "You know JJ - quick instincts. He reached for his gun as soon as he saw the other guy reach for his. They fired at the same time. The other guy came off worse. Just as well JJ fired, as the con would have kept going until JJ was dead."

"Did JJ kill him?"

"Critical condition. I believe they're waiting on his family to make the decision on switching him off."

I took a moment to let the drama sink in, sat back and let out a long breath. "Geez. Good old JJ. Anyone else and they'd have been a goner."

"Well, that's the reason I needed to speak with you. JJ's going to make a full recovery, but until then, I'm assigning you a new partner."

"Alright."

"I want you to work with Winston. I hear you guys are close."

"That's right. We trained together."

"Did more than that together before you joined the force, or so I hear." Sandra fixed me with a knowing look so intense that I felt the hairs on the back of my neck stand up and I shifted uncomfortable in my check.

"I heard those records got expunged."

"I have my sources."

"It was a scheme they were running at the time – expunging records for under-sixteens that didn't reoffend within two years and joined the mentor program."

"I remember it. I thought it was a stupid idea." She looked at me, and then smiled. "I'm pleased to say that I was wrong. I've put my name to a number of similar programs since then. A criminal record is one of the reasons so many young offenders reoffend – that black mark on their record follows them everywhere; it makes it hard to get honest work."

"I sure as hell wouldn't have been able to join the force if somebody hadn't given me that second chance."

"I knew about it when I hired you, of course."

"You did? Then why'd you take the chance?"

"Curiosity, mostly."

I sighed. "I was a stupid kid back then."

"Real stupid."

I could only imagine what Captain Russell had thought of me back then. From what I heard, she hated her own father who had always chosen the life of crime and made her own life dangerous for her when she was young. Everybody who'd knocked on the door of her childhood home had been looking for a gun. It had been a scary upbringing. And then there I'd been, with a conviction for armed robbery. It made me respect her even more, that she'd given me a second chance, despite her hatred for guns and the people who toyed with them.

"Anyway," Sandra continued, "I've decided that I want you two together for now. You grew up here. You know this community. You're probably the best person to show Winston the ropes. I don't think he's used to real policing."

I held back a snicker. It would be offensive to Winston to say that the work he'd done before he transferred wasn't real policing, but I think that those of us who were true to policing the hood believed that there was a difference. There was something about knowing that there was a very real chance you'd die in the line of duty any day that made the job seem real. If there wasn't a chance that you were gonna get shot and die that day, then you might as well be a pencil-pusher in any nine-to-five office job.

"He ain't soft," I told her. "We were born and raised here. Nobody that survived childhood in this community is soft."

"He was soft enough not to stay," Sandra challenged. "I looked at his transfer file. Never fired a weapon in the line of duty. Minimal arrests. No major incidents. Either he lived in the dullest town in the world, or he avoided real conflict."

"I worked there for a while. It's a pretty dull place."

"Ah yes, your own transfer. I must say that I was disappointed when I received the request. I didn't peg you for one of the ones to run away."

"I came back, didn't I?"

"Ah, yes. So, it was just a break then?"

"Something like that."

"I know this job is hard, Reggie, and I know that you don't shy away. You've seen the worst that this place has to offer, and after what happened with that principal's little girl... I do understand that this place can get too much. We joke about soft cops, but I don't think you're soft if you need to step back sometimes. In fact, sometimes a cop has got to step back. The only thing worse than a soft cop is a cop on the edge of a breakdown, and I've seen too many break down. I'm glad you left us for a while, Reg... but I'm glad you came back."

Here we were, rolling together again. When I'd first joined the academy, this had been my dream – me and Winston saving our community together. Winston was here at last, but I could tell that he was uncomfortable patrolling some of the darker and dirtier streets of the hood. He looked out the window as I drove slowly through the streets and pulled a face at everything he saw going on outside.

"Reggie, it's every street corner in this place, isn't it? Where do we even begin?"

"52nd and Howard," I told him. "That's where someone's most likely to get shot down. I usually center my beat around that corner and then make a move if something gets radioed in."

"I can't believe you've been doing this for all this time. I know it was our dream once and everything, but don't you ever get tired of this place?"

"Every day. But you know, there's just enough adrenalin in the job to wake me up again."

"Have you told Rosie about JJ?"

"No. You know how she'd worry."

"No, I kept my lips shut on that one as well. Elizabeth hates that I'm even here. She went mad when I filed the transfer. She couldn't understand it."

"What did you tell her?"

"That I had unfinished business."

"It's hard for them to understand, if they didn't grow up here."

"Rosie understands it."

I shook my head. "No, I don't think she does understand it. She knows I have a cause, and that's enough for her to accept that this is what I've got to do, but she still tells me nearly every day about how much she'd like to pick up and move to the country."

"Would you ever do it?"

"Maybe one day. But, it's like you said – unfinished business."

We carried on driving slowly around the 'hood. Winston kept watching the ghetto roll by with this look of nostalgia on his face. "It was tough growing up here, wasn't it?"

"Yeah, it was."

"You do gotta feel sorry for these kids."

"Yeah, you do."

"Until they grow up and get guns and start killing people, then you don't feel so sorry for them no more."

"That's just the thing, though, ain't it, Winston? You gotta make the changes early. Plant the seed in their minds. Inspire them. Give them some hope."

"I remember what it was like to feel that angry. That's why so many of them do so much bad shit. Anger."

"I remember too."

"Leo was angrier than either of us."

"His parents weren't around at all. I mean, ours weren't around, but at least they weren't around for the right reasons."

"Makes you wonder what we'd have been if we'd have been born anywhere else in the world. What would Leo have done if he'd lived just a bit longer?"

"He'd have been a good dad. I know that much."

"Yeah, he would've been, wouldn't he? He'd have been fun."

"He'd have been loyal."

"I miss that guy."

"Me too."

It felt strange to talk about Leo with Winston, here, now, in this community again. We'd talked about him before, but it had never felt so sad. I guess it was because here we were, living our dreams, that we'd spoken about for so long after we'd done our time, and had worked so hard to make it happen, and it just kind of brought it home that two of us were doing what we'd planned, but one of us hadn't made it. We used to be three.

"You know, I reckon Leo would've made a good cop," Winston told me. "Not like us, though. An undercover cop. Can you imagine? He'd get all the fun of getting up to no good, but none of the trouble."

I smiled to think about it. Yeah, that would have suited Leo down to the ground. He'd get to roam the streets seeing it all go down and mouthing off as much as he liked, and it would only have made him fit in and get the job done.

"The three of us still together. Yeah, that would've been something."

"How's Shannon doing?"

"She's off the radar. I think she's gone back to wherever she was before I called her back."

"And Flo?"

"She's doing well under her new care plan. Sad story, but we'll all get old one day."

"I haven't heard you talk about Randall in a while."

"I'm trying to let it go – like you told me. I got in touch with Gina, and that's it. I don't know what else I can do."

"It's a tough one." Winston mused. "Did you think any more about maybe bringing him in?"

"You know, I don't think Randall would learn anything from being inside. I think he'd only get ideas and make new contacts. He's too determined to be on the wrong side of the law. He wants to cause trouble."

"Just like Leo."

"Yup, just like Leo."

"Still, at least we're here now, right? It just goes to show that people can make it out alive – sort of. We're still here, I mean, in this place- but we're surviving."

CHAPTER THIRTY-ONE

I t was eleven 'o'clock, so me and Winston were at the little café at the end of 52nd street to pick up some coffee, as we always did. Then we took five to stand just outside the doors and take a breather. It didn't last for long. As we were standing there, a young man came shooting past at full speed and seconds later five other young men followed in close pursuit.

Winston and me looked at each other and immediately knew that something heavy was going down. We both chucked our coffees into the trash can opposite and raced back to our vehicle so we could catch up with the chase. We followed the chase to a back alley, our sirens blaring.

The five guys who'd been chasing the young man scattered when they realised there were cops on the scene, which left just the one young man who'd been ahead of the group. He'd gone running down the alley, only to find that he'd hit a dead end and was now stuck there with a cop car blocking his exit.

I exited the vehicle with my hand on my holster and Winston just behind me and slowly approached the runner. As I got closer, I realised that the young man was Randall. I felt a moral dilemma rush over me, because I couldn't avoid this situation any longer. Randall was in trouble and I needed to start treating him like every other kid in this town and make him face the consequences of his actions. It became even more clear that I was going to have to take him in and follow through on the law when a couple more cop cars pulled up behind us. The chase had obviously been witnessed by the whole community and somebody had called it in. Now there was a group of us blues all surrounding Randall, and I was at the head of it all.

He was shaking wildly and clutching a large carefully wrapped bundle to his chest. His brown eyes were wide open and frantic. He was breathing heavily from running so fast. There were beads of sweat dripping down his forehead. I held out my hands in a calming gesture.

"Relax, Randall. It's OK. What you got there?"

The question was barely out of my mouth before Randall pulled out a gun from the waistband of his pants and pointed it at me threateningly. Like somebody had flicked a switch, every police officer pulled out their own guns in response and pointed them at Randall. I was the only one who didn't reach for his gun. Instead, I kept my eyes fixed closely on Randall and took a step closer.

"I can tell you're in some serious trouble now, but I can help you."

"Enough, Reggie!" Randall yelled at me in a choked voice. "You can't help me! When you gonna understand that? There ain't nothing you can do!"

"Tell me what's going on here."

"They're after me – that's what's going on! Now I'm here and they're gonna get to me somehow."

"Nobody's gonna get to you."

"They got friends on the inside. If you put me away, they'll get me. If you let me walk, they get me. I had a job to do, and you just got in the way and now I'm dead."

"You're not talking to some street thug, Randall. I'm someone who can help."

"That badge don't give you no power out there. Not you or nobody else can be watching every second of the day, and as soon as your back is turned, they're gonna get me."

"Put down the gun, Randall. There's no need for that."

Randall only raised the barrel higher in response; his face pulled back in an ugly scowl. "Don't tell me what to do." The hand that wasn't on the gun he put to his head and he grimaced like his head was splitting open.

I'd been where he was and I knew that feeling that came over you when you realised you'd screwed up bad and there was no way out; when you'd finally taken it too far and had no choice but to see where you'd end up next.

"It's not over. Put the gun down. Give yourself up quietly. You'll get a better deal then. I know you're not the mastermind behind any of this, Randall. We can work together, you and me. I can get you help."

"What, if I rat on Butch or somebody else? You just don't get it, Reggie. I tell you I'm dead, and you want to make me deader. You talk about how you remember the streets and you know what it's like, but it seems to me you've forgotten real fast if you think it's that easy to walk away when you're in this deep. I've made promises to the sorts of people who don't take broken promises lightly."

"We'll get to that," I promised him. "But it's got to start with putting the gun down."

"It would be you, wouldn't it?" Randall scowled. "It would be you here now. This all started with you! If my dad had been here…"

"You never knew him, Randall. But I did. Trust me, if he'd have been here, it wouldn't have been much different. He was trouble."

"Just like me."

"It don't have to be that way."

"It's too late."

"You still have a choice."

For some reason, those words made Randall lose it and he straightened his arm out solid and his finger began to pull back on the trigger.

I heard the shot fire and raised my arm to shield my face, waiting to feel the bullet tear through me. Except, the pain didn't come. The blood didn't spill. I didn't feel a thing. I opened my eyes and realised that the bullet hadn't come from Randall's gun. No, Randall was lying on the ground with blood gushing out his neck. I turned to my left. Sure enough, there was Winston with his eyes wide and shocked and his hand shaking against the handle of a revolver. He'd fired.

"What have I done?" he whispered.

I didn't have time to reply to him then. Instead, we needed to secure the scene. That meant officers in action. One officer rushed to kick the gun away from Randall's hand. When it was clear away, we could approach him. Once again, I was the one with my hands over the wound, but I knew that it was too late. Randall was already turning cold.

I could see where the bullet had hit him right in the neck, no doubt straight through the jugular. There was blood everywhere. A river of it. I was kneeling in the pool of his blood and I could feel it soaking through to my skin. Randall's eyes were frozen open, staring upwards; all signs of life gone.

We did what we were meant to do and called the EMTs, but all of us knew that it was just pointless routine. Randall was dead. Shot down by one of our own.

Another officer, Mark, gripped Winston's shoulder reassuringly. "He was gonna pull that trigger, Winston. You did the right thing. It takes guts to make that kind of call. You're a true blue."

Winston didn't respond to that. He just looked kind of numb and handed the gun to the officer who had just spoken to him, like he didn't want it near him anymore, and then he walked away. I followed him.

"He's right, you know, Winston. This is not your fault."

"I just killed Leo's son." Winston's words were quiet, soft. His face was full of sorrow. His shoulders were hunched over and he just looked so... defeated. Now, I'd expected Randall to get shot sooner or later, and I'd thought that when that time came, I'd have no sympathy for the shooter, but now it had happened, I couldn't blame Winston for what had happened.

"You saved my life, Winston."

"He was just a kid."

I didn't really know what else to say. Death by cop was not an unusual way for these kids to go out, unfortunately. It happened all the time when somebody got cornered and refused to back down. The fear in them was so great that they would die, when me and Winston knew better than anybody that anybody could come back from their worst behaviour if they wanted it enough. Others would choose to die a so-called legend then live an ordinary life.

I was so worried for Winston and so swept up in all the debriefings and investigations and interviews and paperwork that followed for the next few days that I didn't really have time to feel anything at first. I think my own emotions hit me when I finally went to see Shannon a few days after Leo's death. I hadn't been the one to deliver the news of her son's death, but I knew I'd have to face her eventually.

Somebody else had tracked her down to where she'd been staying, and she'd come back to Flo's in preparation for Randall's funeral. I met her there that day. She was sitting in the lounge with a cigarette in one hand and a vodka in the other, with her hair an unwashed mess and her eyes red, but her expression numb.

I sat down near her and didn't say anything for a while. When I did speak, my voice was low and full of regret. "I'm so sorry, Shannon."

She blinked, and a single tear rolled down her cheek. "I thought you were gonna protect him."

"I thought so too."

"But you were there when it happened. Why did you let him pull the trigger?"

"It was police instinct. Randall was gonna shoot."

"He was aiming it at you, right?"

"Yeah."

"He always did blame you for what happened with Leo."

"Yeah, I know."

Shannon sniffed and wiped her eyes with the back of her hand. "They're both gone now. First Leo, and now my son. He's gone out just like his father, and I did nothing to save him."

Every one of us was carrying a guilty conscience now. Me, because my mission to save Randall had ended in death. Winston, because he'd been the one to pull the trigger. Shannon, because she didn't do enough to lead him down a different path from the start.

I was trying not to blame anyone, even though I felt like it was partly my fault. The thing is, what I'd learned from this year, was that

CHRISTOPHER M. SPENCE

these things are bigger than just one person or just one choice made on one day. They are the accumulation of the poison in a community, the poison in a whole life and a series of bad, bad decisions. Sure, we can say that Winston pulled the trigger and that's the whole story, but that would be leaving out a whole lot of facts. The story's much longer than that. Randall died from a bullet to the neck, but he died because of the issues of the community he lived in. He died because he was afraid of what would happen if he lived. He died because he was angry. He died because he was trying to fit into a culture of gun violence and despair.

Had we done enough to try and stop it from getting to this point? Who could say? I felt devastated that Randall had died too much like Leo, but I also felt like I had done everything I could. It wasn't enough, but it was everything I could do. To me, that meant that I needed to make sure that next time I could do more. That meant investing time, energy and resources into initiatives like the Polly Foundation. That meant working on my career to get higher and higher up the ladder so that I could support others to this role. That meant growing stronger, more determined and more resilient. This time it hadn't been enough, but maybe next time I could do more.

It was a sad and sobering thought to know for sure that there *would be* a next time. Randall was not the first and he certainly would not be the last kid needing to be pushed in the right direction and saved from himself and the dangerous beckoning of the ghetto. There would be other kids, with other issues that would need me someday.

Investigation after Randall's death brought more of the story to life. It turns out that he'd been taking a lot of drugs on Butch's dime and hadn't been able to pay it back. His life was on the line if he couldn't pay the debt. Butch had offered him one final out. He'd heard that a rival gang had a big drug deal about to go down. Randall's job was to pose as the buyer and then steal the package – a huge amount of cocaine. He'd managed to get his hands on the package, but he hadn't got far. The gang had chased him.

186

Once I heard more of the story, I knew for sure that whether we had been there that day or not, that Randall would have died the same way. If he had failed to steal the drugs, then Butch would have done him in. If he had succeeded, then the rival gang would have tracked him down. Randall had made himself a lot of enemies, even within his own crowd, and sooner or later, he would have run out of luck.

I felt sorry for Randall, because I knew that he'd been a troubled kid who'd let things spiral out of control. Joining Butch's gang had all started as a way to feel like he had friends around him, which he needed considering his grandmother hadn't been herself and his mom was in a state. It had given him excitement, and a sense of purpose, because they had jobs for him to do. It had made him feel important when he did something right.

I remembered that feeling. It was why I had done the things that I had done when I was young. There was a buzz that you got when your gang patted you on the back and said you were the man; that you were one of them. When you were young, lonely and stuck in a dead-end community, that feeling was everything.

But Randall had let it get out of control because he'd been reckless. He'd taken the teaser drugs that Butch had given him without thinking about what the catch might be. Then, once he got hooked and couldn't keep up with paying for what he was taking, he'd got himself trapped. Then Butch had him right where he wanted him.

I'd been lucky that the 'gang' I'd chosen to roll with had only been a group of young kids trying to impress each other. Randall had fallen in with older boys with darker intentions. They were an established gang with established rivalries and big money to be made. They weren't kids messing around. They were big names in a small town, and Randall had got caught up in their chaos and been the one to pay the price. His biggest crime had been naivety.

I did feel sad about Randall's death, but, surprisingly, it didn't haunt me as much as I'd thought it would have, and I think it's because I'd come to terms with my own limits over the last year. I'd come to understand the hood and all its wicked ways, and learned that I was one tiny, tiny cog in a giant, corrupt machine and that I couldn't take responsibility for everything that went wrong on my watch, because I wasn't the only cog that spinning. I couldn't say that I missed Randall all that much, because all the while I'd tried to save him, I'd not really got to know him. That was one mistake that I took responsibility for. I'd let Randall become a symbol of what I was trying to achieve, rather than recognising him as an individual kid with his own worries and insecurities and wants and needs and dreams. I'd made him a mission, and maybe that was why I'd never truly been able to connect with him. I wouldn't make that mistake again. I wouldn't treat the next kid like a re-run. Sure, I'd seen it a thousand times before – the same old story; I'd lived it, right? – but, to these kids, it was all new and scary and belonging felt like it meant everything.

I'd learned a damned lot this year, but I knew there was still a lot more I had to learn and a lot I had yet to understand. It was like Charlie had always told me – you've got to keep learning, keep persevering; you've got to make yourself the person you need. That might take time, and I was ready to fail a lot, but I was also determined that I was gonna make all the difference I could make for as long as I was here.

CHAPTER THIRTY-TWO

t was a cheap funeral with cheap eulogies. There was nobody there who really cared about Randall to have much to say about his death, or about his life. Flo came, but I don't think she really understood what had happened or what was going on – she was in fast decline. Shannon was there, but she didn't have much to say. There were few special memories between her and Randall, because she'd spent so much of her time with him passed out or drugged up. I'd not taken the time to get to know him, because all I'd cared about was redeeming myself for Leo's death; and so, here we were, saying goodbye to a young man that none of us had really known. In the absence of a better speaker, I had a go at speaking for him at the funeral.

"It's hard to know what to say about Randall that can make this day any easier or that can bring much meaning to his death." I was standing at the podium in the church in the same black suit I'd worn to Charlie's funeral and I felt nervous in front of the small congregation. I caught eyes with Rosie in the front row and she smiled encouragingly. "Randall's story is a sad one. He was a young man with a lot of emotion, a lot of determination, a lot of grit. He reminded me a lot of his father, who was a good friend. Like his father, he died too soon, and I don't know what I can say about that. It shouldn't have happened the way it did, but it happened. I wish I could say more about the kind of guy that Randall was, or what he achieved in his life, but I didn't know him well enough to be able to do him justice. Yet, he was important to me, because he represented all the young men out there. He struggled with the same issues that they struggled with, and faced the same obstacles. So, although I can't do him justice now, I can make him the promise that what I have learned from his life and his death will go with me always. I will never stop trying, Randall, to make changes; to make progress. Please forgive us all for the things we didn't do."

It was short and it was insufficient, but nobody had anything else to say. We filled up the rest of the ceremony with hymns and poems printed from offline. We'd wanted to play his favourite rap song, but it had seemed unfitting in a church. So, really, there was nothing of Randall in his final goodbye.

After his coffin had been lowered into the ground, I took some time to speak to him alone. There he was, next to Leo.

"I'm sorry, Randall," I said to the earth. "I'm sorry that this is your big goodbye. I'm sorry that nobody really came. I'm sorry that the people who are here had nothing really to say. That says as much about us as it says about you. We're people who focus on reputation and glory and our own goals, rather than on people. If we'd have taken more time to know you and why you did the things you did and what was going on in your head, then maybe we'd have had a better idea of how to get through to you when you really needed us to. I'm sorry for that. I know you always hated when I spoke about choices, but I want you to know that I recognise that there were so many choices you couldn't make. You were born to Shannon and Leo, and neither were there for you. That wasn't your fault. You were let down. I'll keep fighting for you, and all the others to try and make this place better. I know it's not much when you're gone, but it's all I can do for you now."

Winston hadn't attended the service, but I saw him pull up in his car and make his way now over to the grave. Everybody else had moved onto the reception, but I'd wanted a chance to say my own goodbye. Winston must have felt the same.

"I didn't think you'd come."

"I didn't think I'd be welcome."

I didn't know what to say. Winston had pulled the trigger, but he hadn't killed Randall. Randall had decided his fate when he'd gone to pull the trigger.

"You once told me that if Randall ended up this way, it would have been his own fault."

"That was back when I didn't know that I'd be the one who pulled the trigger."

"It's still true, though. He made his decision. Even at the very end, we were there telling him that there was another way, but he didn't want to hear it."

"I can't blame him, though. He had Butch and that gang on his tail. I'd have been scared, too."

"Yeah. I feel sorry for him."

"Me too. Don't seem right that father and son are there lying side by side. Barely two years between how old they were when they died."

"History tends to repeat itself in these parts."

"That's why I'm leaving," Winston told me firmly, turning to look at me with a serious and sad expression hanging in his tired eyes. "This life ain't for me."

"Where are you going?"

"Back to my old beat. I want the quiet life, Reggie. I know that you feel spurred on when these things happen, but I just feel tired. If this one was a one-off, I could take it, but I know it's not. It's gonna happen again and again and again, and I can't keep watching kids die. I won't shoot another one, and that's what it comes down to. I know in my own head that I won't have it in me to make that call again, but I know, that if I stay, the day'll come when I've got to. So, I'm leaving. Call me soft if you want, but I don't see the glory in the work that needs to be done here."

I patted his back in acknowledgement. "You're not soft. I've seen cops have to make some tough calls in my time, but that's the toughest call I've ever seen. It came down to me or Randall."

"It wasn't a choice. It was reflex."

"Still, you saved my life. I know you feel guilt, Winston, and there's not a lot I can do to make you feel better, but I can make you a promise: I won't waste the gift you've given me. I'm gonna stay here and make whatever difference I can make."

Winston nodded slowly. "I know I give you a hard time for being an idealist and still believing that change can happen, but I'm kinda glad that someone believes it. Otherwise you're just two ex-cons staring at two graves, just waiting for it to happen all over again. It would be nice to think that somewhere down the line there might be an end to all this."

"It might not be in our lifetime," I said. "I know I might never live to see this place brought to life, but these things take time. It won't happen overnight. It's got to be a lot of small changes over a long time, but someone's gotta start the ball rolling. It starts today."

CHAPTER THIRTY-THREE

From the beginning of this story to the end, not much has changed. You're probably wondering why I even told this story when we all know that it's not the end. There will be another Randall – many more kids will come and go and be victims to stubbornness, naivety and a vicious community. And when I go, there will be another Reggie to fight for them. There will be other Pollys and other Freds. Other Charlies and other Winstons. But just because a story's been told so many times, does that mean it shouldn't be told again?

When Polly died, Mr Branch told her story because he said he was an educator, and there was a lesson to be learned. I guess that's the same reason I'm telling my story, too. There are things to be taken from it; things that I've discovered; lessons that I've learned.

I've learned that one man can do both so little and so much. The choices I make today might not change the world tomorrow – but they will change the world. You see, a good choice has a ripple effect and you will never have the vision to see how far that ripple spreads.

Sometimes it is only by looking back over a story like this that we can understand that concept. If I had chosen not to rob that factory in my own youth, maybe Leo wouldn't have gone to prison, maybe he wouldn't have died, maybe he would have been there to raise his son and been a salesman, maybe Randall wouldn't have gone off the rails, and maybe he'd be alive. Maybe if Leo hadn't mouthed off to the wrong person in prison, he wouldn't have been stabbed and maybe he'd have walked out on his release date and been there for

Randall, and Randall wouldn't have gone looking for companionship and understanding in a gang, and Randall would be alive. Maybe if Randall hadn't accepted that first teaser drug from Butch, he wouldn't have got hooked and wouldn't have built up a debt and wouldn't have had to risk his life to make it right and maybe he'd be alive. Maybe if Shannon hadn't started drinking and paid attention to her boy, he never would have come back to the hood and he would never have met Cody and Butch and he would still be alive.

You see, there were so many people who made so many choices that all seemed so small at the time. None of them could have foreseen how those ripples would have spread and lead to death. Now, no one person is responsible for the whole lake, but we're all responsible for our own ripples, and we're all swimming in that same water.

Now, I'm not one for big metaphors and fancy ways of explaining big ideas, so maybe all of that makes no sense at all. I don't know. All I know is that I've come to learn that my choices matter. Caring about other people matters. Caring about my community matters.

When I was young, I didn't realise any of that. I felt small and forgotten and like nothing I did was important. God, if I had realised just what might happen decades down the line to myself and other people just because I did what I had to do… maybe I'd have thought twice. Yeah, I tell my story because there is a lesson to be learned here.

If there is any kind of ending to this story, I don't know that it's a happy one. The only person I was trying to save is dead and although I talk a lot about cogs and bigger pictures and ripples, I still feel responsible for what happened to Leo, and I'll carry that always. The hood is still fooling people into thinking that there is no escape, and people are still falling for it. My job is to be the one who shouts back.

This story was about my mission to save Randall, but it was also about remembering what my cause was. I didn't manage to save Randall, but I did remember what all of this is for. I'm trying to save my community, one person at a time. But I am only responsible for my own ripples. There is so much more to be done.

ABOUT THE AUTHOR

Christopher M Spence is a renowned educator and dedicated community advocate. His leadership role in working with the broader educational community to manage issues, develop policy and promote causes that benefit youth and achieve measurable results has been widely recognized. The success of these initiatives were featured in a documentary about his life, "Person to Person" and in several articles including an article in Reader's Digest entitled "Man on a Mission."

He is an articulate, knowledgeable and inspirational speaker and is a passionate champion of public outreach, and the important role education plays in the development of individuals and the prosperity of the nation.

He is the author of several books the most recent include SnowBall Brothers4Life, Ice Cold and The Adventures of Bobby Allen. He has devoted his career to advancing innovation in education, providing national and international leadership through invited lectures and participation on national and international roundtable discussions.

Throughout his career, Spence has been dedicated to improving the student experience, creating links to the community, and supporting innovation. He has won many awards for his outstanding contributions to education and the community, including outstanding alumni award from Simon Fraser University, Educational Leader of the Year, Niagara University's College of Education, Phi Delta Kappa Outstanding Educator Award, a John C Holland Award for Professional Achievement, a Harry Jerome Award, a Dare Arts Award and a Harmony Leadership in Education Award.

He also has several film credits to his name: "No J", Teammates, SkinGames, Football's Pioneering Duo, Silence the Violence, Making Waves, She Said: Silence the Violence and Jail or Yale: Young, Black and Out of Options?

Printed in the United States
By Bookmasters